KU-614-921

LOVESWEPT® No. 30
Marcia Evanick
Indescribably Delicious

BANTAM BOOKS
TORONTO · NEW YORK · LONDON · SYDNEY · AUCKLAND

INDESCRIBABLY DELICIOUS

A BANTAM BOOK 0 553 44035 7

First Publication in Great Britain

PRINTING HISTORY
Bantam edition published 1991

Bantam Books are published by Transworld Publishers Ltd., 61–63 Uxbridge Road, Ealing, London W5 5SA, in Australia by Transworld Publishers (Australia) Pty. Ltd., 15–23 Helles Avenue, Moorebank, NSW 2170, and in New Zealand by Transworld Publishers (N.Z.) Ltd., Cnr. Moselle and Waipareira Avenues, Henderson, Auckland.

Printed and bound in Great Britain by
Cox & Wyman Ltd., Reading, Berks.

"Are you sure there's nothing I can help you with?" Dillon asked.

Elizabeth glanced up and smiled at the man who'd been sitting and watching her for twenty minutes. "What are you thinking?"

"How kissable you look."

With trembling hands she set the mixing bowl on the counter and kept beating the batter.

Dillon stood up and walked toward her. She hadn't ordered him from the house, which was a good sign, he decided. She also hadn't run into his arms. When he came up behind her, he gently removed the large bowl from her hands. Carefully turning Elizabeth by her shoulders, he trapped her between the counter and his body. He placed his hands on either side of her, and without touching her, he said, "You're the most beautiful woman I've ever known, inside and out."

"But you barely know me," tumbled from her lips.

"Anyone can see you're beautiful on the outside, but it's the inside that's most important," he said, his finger tracing a line from her cheek to her lower lip.

Elizabeth pulled away and headed for the pantry off the kitchen. When she reached up to grab a pan on the top shelf, Dillon said, "Allow me," his body moving up close behind hers. Elizabeth felt her body trembling at his closeness and her lips quivered in anticipation of his kiss. A moment later, Dillon covered her mouth with his, and the cake pan dropped to the floor. . . .

WHAT ARE *LOVESWEPT* ROMANCES?

They are stories of true romance and touching emotion. We believe those two very important ingredients are constants in our highly sensual and very believable stories in the *LOVESWEPT* line. Our goal is to give you, the reader, stories of consistently high quality that may sometimes make you laugh, sometimes make you cry, but are always fresh and creative and contain many delightful surprises within their pages.

Most romance fans read an enormous number of books. Those they truly love, they keep. Others may be traded with friends and soon forgotten. We hope that each *LOVESWEPT* romance will be a treasure—a "keeper." We will always try to publish

LOVE STORIES YOU'LL NEVER FORGET
BY AUTHORS YOU'LL ALWAYS REMEMBER

The Editors

To my mother, Ruth Henderson,
who's always there.

Love

One

Elizabeth blinked her eyes, trying desperately to believe what was in front of her. There in the middle of her prized pansies sat the mangiest dog she had ever seen. She quickly glanced around her small backyard, hoping to see the animal's owner. The yard was empty. Great, now what was she supposed to do?

She stood and took a hesitant step toward her squashed pansies, waving her arms. "Go home. Get going." The dog wagged its tail in response, wiping out another geranium. Elizabeth groaned. She wasn't positive but she'd swear the dog actually smiled. Carefully placing her trowel and cultivator on the ground, she called to the dog, "Come here, boy. Come on."

Her mouth fell open as the animal looked away from her and started to munch on her award-winning pansies. Total fury swept through her as she watched weeks' worth of hard work being gobbled up by a flea-bit hair ball. She marched over to the small animal and picked him up. "Stop that. Bad doggie." The animal looked at her with his big brown eyes as he licked his chops and belched. She was so startled that her grip almost slipped. Not only was he untrained, he was rude.

Well, at least he seemed friendly. She tried to keep the muddy paws away from her clean blouse as she carried the dog around the side of the house.

"Gee, Mom, where did you get the dog?"

Elizabeth smiled down at her seven-year-old son, Aaron. "I found him in the garden eating my pansies."

"Can we keep him?"

"No."

Her son's brown eyes silently pleaded as one softly spoken word escaped his lips. "Please?"

Elizabeth sighed deeply. Why did being a parent mean saying no so often? "I'm sorry, Aaron, but you can't keep him. We already have a cat. Cats and dogs don't get along." Seeing a sad look in her son's eyes, she added, "I'm sure he already belongs to someone."

Carefully studying the small dog, she shook her head. Who would want to claim that mangy mutt? Someone obviously owned him. Even though his ancestry was indeterminable, he seemed to be in good health. "How about helping me find his owner?"

"If no one claims him, can we keep him?"

"No."

With downcast eyes Aaron followed her around the side of the house, and when she came to an abrupt halt, he walked right into her back. Elizabeth felt Aaron knock into her, but she was more interested in what was going on at the house next door. A large moving van was parked out front, and it was clear people were finally moving in.

The huge Victorian had stood empty for nearly two years, ever since Doc Snyder had passed on. Though she'd often seen realtors at the house, a buyer was hard to find. Not only was it the largest, most magnificent house in town, but it was also the most expensive. A couple of months earlier Elizabeth had heard that an architect and his family had purchased the house. It looked like she was finally going to get new neighbors.

After repositioning her grip on the small bundle of fur in her arms, she walked toward the yellow moving van. A small parade of men was busy carrying furniture and boxes. After a quick glance she realized her new neighbors hadn't arrived yet, only the moving men, in their seemingly proscribed uniform of jeans, T-shirts, and battered sneakers. Maybe the dog belonged to one of them, she thought. She decided to ask their foreman.

After dismissing the two men wearing gold earrings and ponytails as helpers, she turned her attention to a third man leaving the van carrying a wooden kitchen chair in each arm. With a pleasant smile she started walking toward him to ask about the dog. Her voice died as she read the lewd slogan on the front of his T-shirt. There was no way his shirt pertained to surfing. Fiery red stained her cheeks as the handsome young red-haired man smiled at her.

Dillon McKenzie had just finished lecturing his two sons on their moving-day responsibilities. Earlier he had assigned Kevin and Kyle the job of watching Rufus, the family dog, while he moved furniture. Now Rufus was missing and probably up to no good. Dillon was headed out the front door trying to decide whether he should continue to help his younger brother, Shane, and his two friends move furniture or go looking for Rufus when he heard a woman's voice.

He had gone only two steps out the door when all thoughts of trying to salvage the day slid into a black hole, never to be seen again. Shane stood

next to the moving van with his chest puffed out,
biceps bulging, and a lascivious smile curving his
lips. Not ten feet away stood a woman clutching
Rufus, with a small boy half-hidden behind her.

As Dillon moved off the porch he noticed the
blush on the woman's cheeks and glared at his
brother. Obviously, she'd read the slogan on his
shirt. When he'd showed up at five o'clock that
morning, Dillon had asked Shane to change it,
but his brother had just shrugged and explained
it would liven up the small town where Dillon had
chosen to move.

Out of the corner of her eye Elizabeth saw another man come from the house and quickly turned
toward him. Her first impression was the man
was tall. He was older than the other three, probably in his middle thirties, with thick reddish-brown
hair that gleamed in the sunlight and clear green
eyes that sparkled with friendliness. Outwardly
he appeared normal. He wasn't wearing an ear-
ring or a ponytail, and there was no suggestive
saying printed on his chest. She hoped he was
the boss. Seeing his apologetic smile brought a
tentative one to her lips. "Excuse me, but do you
know whom this dog belongs to?"

Dillon's smile slipped a notch at the sound of
her soft feminine voice. Large brown eyes stared
uncertainly out of a face that was as fresh and
clean as the country air he was breathing. A long,
dark brown braid hung down her back and ended
at her waist. His eyes traveled down from her
well-worn jeans to her sparkling white sneakers.
Pure male appreciation shone in his eyes as he
reached out for the mud-covered Rufus. "Yes,
ma'am. He lives here."

As Dillon lifted Rufus from her arms he studied
the dirty paw prints that now covered the front of
her yellow blouse. Heat surfaced low in his stomach as he watched her womanly breast rise and

fall in silent irritation. When he raised his head he noticed that embarrassment stained her cheeks and anger glittered in her dark eyes.

Elizabeth watched the man in shock. She couldn't believe his rudeness! Here she was doing a good deed, and what did she get in return? A Romeo who broadcasted his intentions across his chest, a pair of gypsies, and Mr. Mountain who went speechless at the sight of dirty laundry. Seething with anger, mostly directed at herself for allowing them to bother her, she mumbled a hasty, "Goodbye."

Dillon watched as the small boy took two tentative steps after his mother, then turned and stopped. "He ate my mom's pansies."

"He did?" Dillon tried to inject some surprise into his voice. Nothing Rufus did shocked him anymore.

"Aaron."

"Coming."

Dillon watched as mother and son walked back to the small cottage next door. Painted white with red shutters, the house would have seemed plain if it were not for the beds of colorful flowers growing in neat clusters around it. The background disappeared as he concentrated on the dark brown braid, which with every swing gently bumped into a pair of gardening gloves sticking out of her back pocket.

"Uhhh, nice gloves."

Dillon glared at his younger brother. "Shut up, Shane."

Shane raised an eyebrow. "I was just commenting on your new neighbor."

"I know what you were talking about. I don't think her husband would appreciate your thoughts."

"She's not married."

Surprised, Dillon asked, "How do you know?"

"No ring."

Dillon laughed. "What does that prove? With your luck her husband would make the Incredible Hulk look tame. He probably heard your comment on his wife's . . . uh, gloves and is planning to shove the moving van down your throat."

A smile crossed Shane's lips. "I suddenly approve of your choice of towns. I had my doubts in the beginning, but things are definitely looking up around here." He hoisted up the chairs to one of the other movers and headed for the porch. "A woman like that would wear a wedding band if she had one," he said as he walked away.

Dillon shifted Rufus away from his ear as he stared at the house next door where the woman and boy had disappeared. How would his little brother know anything about a woman like that? Shane was the official partygoer. He had partied his way through college and graduated with a B.A. in engineering and blondes. He'd served two years in the Peace Corps in some forsaken country that wasn't even on the map. He'd returned home bearded, tan, and sporting a smile that didn't quite reach his eyes. So what did he know about the type of woman who would wear a wedding band?

Shaking his head and scratching Rufus behind the ears, Dillon made his way back into the house. Damn, he didn't even know her name. For that matter, he'd never introduced himself. Wouldn't *she* be surprised when he finally introduced himself? And wouldn't *he* be surprised when her husband busted him one in the chops. With a disgusted oath at himself and the muddy dog in his arms, he bellowed, "Kyle. Kevin. Come get your dog."

By the time Elizabeth made it to the kitchen she was almost calm. Almost. She knew she really should be thrilled by the attention. It certainly wasn't every day a man stared at her with desire in his eyes. But had it been desire? How was she supposed to know? No man had ever desired her before, not even her husband. Maybe the moving man had a blood deficiency that caused his eyes to wander.

Reaching up into a cabinet, she took down a canister of flour. If she were honest with herself, she'd have to admit it wasn't Mr. Mountain she was mad at but herself. When a spark of interest entered into his green eyes an amazing thing had occurred. She'd responded as a woman.

Elizabeth opened the refrigerator and pulled out a carton of eggs and placed them on the counter. A frown marred her brow as she thought about her ex-husband. At twenty-one she had been swept off her feet by Ron, a handsome man who proclaimed she was his world. After six months of marriage she had found herself divorced, pregnant, and living with her grandparents. Ron had left for a more exciting woman, one that knew how to live.

"What you making, Mom?" Aaron asked as he walked into the room.

Pride filled her heart as she looked at her son. All feelings of hatred toward her ex-husband disappeared. He did manage to accomplish one decent thing in his life—he helped create Aaron. "I'm going to make a cake for the new neighbors."

"Why? Are they hungry?"

"No. This afternoon, when the moving men leave and our new neighbors arrive, we'll go over and introduce ourselves."

A smile split across Aaron's face. "Then we eat cake?"

"No, Aaron. The cake's for them. It's a welcome-to-the-neighborhood present." Seeing the look of disappointment, she added quickly, "Don't you remember what day it is?"

"Pizza!"

Reaching for a large bowl, Elizabeth smiled at her son. It had become a weekly event to go for pizza every Saturday night. Ever since a small pizza parlor had opened in town a few years back, Aaron had an uncontrollable appetite for pizza. An agreement was quickly reached between mother and son. If Aaron was a good boy during the week, kept his room neat, and didn't bother her while she was in the kitchen, they would go for pizza on Saturday night. Who was she kidding? Aaron was always a good boy. He never misbehaved. He was quiet, studious, and never got dirty.

Combining the ingredients with an electric mixer, Elizabeth watched her son as he sat at the kitchen table drawing a picture. Last week had been the end of the school year, and Aaron had completed first grade with straight A's. Pride had shown in her eyes as she read his report card. A trip to the local toy store had netted him two new dinosaur books, his choice not hers. She'd tried talking him into a baseball glove or a skin-diver's plastic mask for the pool this summer, only to be told he wanted the books.

As she poured the batter into the prepared pans a frown marred her face. Was being raised with no male influence making Aaron too serious? His grandfather had passed away when Aaron was only two, and his father had never laid eyes on him.

Elizabeth shook her head as she slid the pans into the oven. She could name a dozen women who would change children with her in a minute. So what was she worried about? Aaron would come out of his shell when he was good and ready.

She walked over to Aaron and stared over his shoulder. "What are you drawing?"

"A picture of that nice dog."

She laughed. "You should have him eating my pansies."

"You're not mad anymore?"

"No. I guess the moving men didn't keep a good eye on him. I'm sure the new neighbors will be able to control him." She gently ruffled her son's light brown hair. "I'm going to change my blouse. After the cake comes out of the oven, how would you like to make some deliveries with me?"

"Okay. Can I help carry some of the boxes for you?"

"Sure. Aren't you my partner?"

"Yep."

The cake was cooling on racks and lunch had been eaten by the time Elizabeth and Aaron drove carefully around town making deliveries. Her home-made cakes, cookies, and chocolates were distributed to residents, shops, and two different farms.

As they turned back into their street she told her son, "It looks like you earned yourself a new pair of sneakers."

"Are we rich yet?"

"Not yet," she said, smiling. "But I'll tell you a secret. We're in the black."

"Black what?"

"It's just a saying, honey. It means for the first time I can stop relying on our inheritance to pay the bills. That means there just might be enough to send you to college after all."

"Do doctors have to go to college?"

"Afraid so, love. For many years."

Watching her son mull over that one, she thought back eight years. She was three months' pregnant when she'd shown up on her grandparents' doorstep. When her parents had been killed in her senior year of high school, her mother's parents took her in and showered her with love. Four years later, again with love and understanding, they gave her back her old room. For the first five months she took a job working as a waitress at a local restaurant.

After Aaron was born she was torn between going back to work to support her son and herself, or staying at home. If she went back to work, she'd have to hire a sitter. Her grandmother was too old to handle an infant eight to ten hours a day.

Five weeks after Aaron was born a neighbor jokingly said he'd pay five bucks for one of her grandmother's indescribably delicious German chocolate cakes. At that moment Elizabeth's business, Indescribably Delicious, was formed. It grew to include cookies and homemade chocolate candies as well. The holidays always produced the most sales and long nights. But the reward was being home with Aaron as he grew up.

As they turned into their driveway she noticed that the moving van was gone from the house next door. A new van sat in the driveway, and bikes and skateboards littered the front yard. With a smile toward the house, Elizabeth said, "Look Aaron, what do you see?"

After unbuckling his seat belt Aaron slid from the car and studied the house next door. "Toys that should have been put away?"

His answer disturbed her more than she cared to admit. "Well, you're partly right. The important thing is toys. That means kids. We're going to have kids for neighbors." Living in an older section of town had its drawbacks. It was peaceful and quiet, but there weren't many playmates for Aaron.

As Elizabeth walked up to her front door she looked around for any signs of the kids or their pansy-eating dog. There were none. She guessed she'd meet them later when she delivered the cake. She hoped there would be at least one boy close to Aaron's age.

An hour later Elizabeth and Aaron slowly made their way up the neighbors' driveway. She carried a triple-decker German chocolate cake, while Aaron held a box of assorted cookies. A cake would have normally been enough, but one look at the assortment of toys spread throughout the yard and Elizabeth was convinced there had to be at least six children.

Climbing the steps to the porch, Elizabeth looked back and smiled at Aaron. He was clearly nervous. Her smile slipped a notch as the sound of shouting voices floated through the screens of the upstairs windows. With a shrug of her shoulders she raised her hand and knocked lightly on the ornamental screen door. From inside she heard the roar of a man's voice. She couldn't make out his words, but he didn't sound pleased. Taking a deep breath she knocked on the door again, more firmly this time.

There was the frantic barking of a dog, followed by a shriek and another bellow from above. With a hesitant glance down at her son she decided that this might not be the best time to deliver a welcome-to-the-neighborhood gift. She was just about to turn away when she heard the sound of young boys' laughter. Firmly planting her feet, she pounded on the door this time. There were boys in the house, and Aaron desperately needed some playmates. And if there were laughter, the roaring giant couldn't be *too* hostile. She hoped.

A moment later a boy with a wild thatch of red hair and a score of freckles opened the screen door. His blue T-shirt was soaked, and there appeared to be shaving cream splattered all over his body. "Hi," he said.

Elizabeth smiled. The boy looked to be the same age as Aaron. "Hi," she said. "Is your mommy or daddy home? I'm Elizabeth Lancaster, and this is my son, Aaron. We live next door and would like to give your family a welcome-to-the-neighborhood present."

He didn't seem to hear her, but his green eyes widened as they lit upon the chocolate cake. "Come on in. I'll get my dad."

Cautiously she entered the house with Aaron close behind. There were piles of furniture and boxes everywhere, and from upstairs the sounds of frantic barking, yelling, and running feet. The chandelier hanging in the formal dining room was swaying slightly. Elizabeth stared up at the ceiling and hoped the plaster would hold. What in the world did they have up there, an elephant?

She was so preoccupied with the upstairs noise that she didn't notice the huge preparatory breath the boy took, until he screamed, "Dad!" The volume almost caused her to drop the cake. She stared at the chaos. Were all the occupants deaf?

The barking grew louder as a giant marshmallow shape came running down the steps. That was it; she was leaving. The entire household was crazy, stark raving mad.

She took a step backward, but the four-legged marshmallow had attached itself to her leg. Raising the cake above her head she shook her leg and stared at the ball of fluff.

A roar from above that sounded like "Rufus" was followed by more pounding on the stairs. Frozen in place, she watched the huge moving man slip on the white foam that covered the stairs and make a loud *thwack* as he hit the cherry banister. Although not one curse word left his mouth, his mood was obvious.

Mr. Mountain was still wearing the same clothes, but now they were covered in white foam. The young boy beside her burst into laughter.

Clearly the family was unstable. All she needed now was to see Uncle Fester coming down the stairs with a light bulb lit in his mouth, and she'd be gone. The giant marshmallow-shaped dog resembled the pansy-eating dog from the morning, but she didn't want to make any assumptions.

The man stood up and walked over to her, groaning. Reaching up with his forearm he swiped at the shaving cream that streaked his jaw. This morning he had seen embarrassment and anger in her face, this afternoon he saw only bafflement. She'd looked like she just walked onto the set of *One Flew Over the Cuckoo's Nest* and didn't know what part she was to play.

Suddenly it dawned on Elizabeth that the "moving man" was her neighbor. She glanced up at the cake she was holding over her head then down at the dog chewing on her shoelace. After a worried glance at her son to see how he was handling the situation, she smiled. Aaron was holding up his box of cookies in imitation of his mother and was grinning from ear to ear.

With a shrug of her shoulders she looked back at Mr. Mountain and smiled her most winning smile. Handing him the cake she said, "Welcome to the neighborhood."

Two

Dillon felt her smile clear down to his soggy toes. He immediately noticed that she and the boy were alone again. Could his brother possibly be right? Was she unmarried? Taking the cake from her and holding it well above the mayhem, Dillon flashed his friendliest smile. "Thank you. Sorry I didn't get a chance to introduce myself this morning, but things, umm . . . seemed to have happened so quickly."

He carefully set the cake down on top of the TV. "I'm Dillon McKenzie. You've already met my son Kyle." There was the sound of feet clopping their way down the stairs, and Dillon's attention turned away from her. "And this is Kevin, my eldest."

Both boys resembled their father in build and hair color, but it ended there. The freckles dusting their smiling faces weren't evident on their dad, and their eyes boasted more gray than green. Still, they looked like your average all-American boys.

Elizabeth heard the pride in Dillon's voice and smiled. He might be crazy as a loon, but he clearly loved his children. "Where are the others?"

"Others?"

"You only have two children?" Her voice was confused.

"At times, two is two too many."

All those toys for two boys, she wondered. Good Lord, either he was filthy rich, or else he spoiled them rotten. "I'm Elizabeth Lancaster and this is my son, Aaron. We live right next door. So if you or Mrs. McKenzie need anything, just come knocking."

"There is no Mrs. McKenzie."

"Oh, I'm sorry." Elizabeth reached for the box Aaron still held over his head and handed it to Dillon. "These are some cookies for you and your boys. I hope you enjoy them."

"I'm sure we will, won't we, boys?"

Elizabeth watched as the older boy, Kevin, eyed the cake as if he hadn't eaten in days. Since they didn't have a mother, it was likely that they might not be accustomed to home-baked goods. She smiled as she turned to go, but Rufus was still attached to her foot.

"Sorry about Rufus there. The boys were giving him a bath."

As far as she could see, the dog was covered with foam. What did they bathe him with, she wondered, a fire extinguisher? She looked back at him with sympathy. The poor man didn't have control over all his faculties. What a shame, all those good looks and muscles, and a mind like chocolate pudding. Doctors probably had a name for it, *puddinosis*. Maybe that's where the name *puddin' head* came from. With a backward look out the screen door, she wondered what time the superintendent was arriving to oversee them. It was quite obvious the family needed supervision.

Dillon correctly read the look in her dark eyes. She thought he was off his rocker. He'd be the first to admit the day hadn't gone according to plan, but moving days seldom went according to plan. And he was not at his best. A headache was starting to form behind his eyes, his shin was black and blue from when he lost an argument with the coffee table, and in the background the refrigerator was making a horrible grinding noise.

After his brother and friends had left, he assigned Kevin and Kyle with the job of washing Rufus. Usually Rufus loved bath time. The dog even had his own rubber duckie. But from the time the boys started to fill the tub, events deteriorated rapidly. The boys could not find any soap, so they lathered poor Rufus with shaving cream. They hadn't turned off the water, so by the time they had finished applying the entire can, the claw-footed tub started to overflow.

Their shouts brought him running. He had entered the bathroom just as Kevin turned off the spigot. With instinct born to fathers who were architects and who knew the damage a flood on a second floor could do, he grabbed the box marked TOWELS and dumped every clean towel in the house on the floor.

Dillon was in the process of soaking up the last of the water when Rufus raced by. Dillon made a wild lunge for the lathered animal as he headed out the bathroom door.

The chase was on. Through bedrooms, down halls, over boxes, and under beds, white foam dotted everything in its path. He would have caught Rufus eventually if it hadn't been for the social call by the woman who stood looking at him as if his cereal was not the only thing that went snap, crackle, pop in the morning.

"The boys couldn't find Rufus's shampoo. They figured shaving cream would work just as well." Sighing, he wondered why he was bothering to explain. She was staring at him as if her son had never misbehaved in his life. "I've been chasing

Rufus for the past five minutes," Dillon continued. "I don't think he wants to finish his bath."

Raising one eyebrow Elizabeth bent over and
picked up the soggy Rufus and handed him to
Dillon.

A tide of red swept up his cheeks as all three
boys burst out laughing. Handing the box of cookies to Kevin, Dillon took the slippery dog and
watched as Elizabeth wiped her hands on the seat
of her jeans.

"Hey, Dad, can Aaron stay here and play?" asked
Kyle.

With a gentle smile Elizabeth answered, "Not
tonight, Kyle. How about tomorrow you and Kevin
come over to our house and give your father a
break."

A smile split Aaron's face showing off his missing two front teeth. "Can they, Mom?"

"Sure. As long as it's okay with their dad."

"Can we, Dad?"

With an amused chuckle, he answered, "As long
as you both behave."

Elizabeth smiled down at the three boys. "Okay,
guys, that's settled. We'll see you tomorrow." With
a friendly smile toward their father, she left saying,
"If you need anything, I'm right next door."

Dillon gripped Rufus tighter as he watched the
faded jeans, streaked with shaving cream, gently
sway across his porch. Why did he have an over-
whelming need to ask if there was a Mr. Lancaster on the scene? He moaned in disgust. He could
picture the introduction now. "Hello, Mr. Lancaster. I'm your new neighbor, Dillon. You have to
excuse me if I act a little funny around your wife. I
seem to have developed this reaction to her."

"Hey, Dad," Kevin said. "Can we have a piece
of cake?"

"No. Let's finish Rufus's bath and get cleaned
up. I'll treat you to a pizza."

• • •

Elizabeth glanced at her menu and listened as her son listed all his plans for the things he wanted to do the next day with his two new friends. She couldn't ever remember seeing him this excited, not even on Christmas Eve. With a loving smile she tried to decide what she was eating for dinner. Every Saturday night Aaron had pizza, while she liked to choose one of Mario's special Italian dinners.

"Hey, Dad, there's Aaron," she heard someone shout across the restaurant.

Startled, Elizabeth looked up and watched as Dillon and his sons entered the small restaurant. A smile and a frantic wave from Aaron brought the boys over to their booth.

A wave of nostalgia hit Dillon as he looked around the pizza parlor. Red vinyl booths lined the outer wall, complete with red-and-white-checkered table cloths and a plastic flower sticking out of a bud vase. A couple of tables were crammed between the two video-game machines and a cooler holding an assortment of soft drinks. A mural of a gondola was on the wall above the booths, and a garland of plastic onions and peppers ran across the far wall. A red neon sign proclaimed to the world that this was MARIO'S. Tomato sauce, cooked sausage, and oregano filled the air with a heavenly aroma. This was why he had moved out to the country—he wanted to give his boys the same type of friendly, comfortable small-time life he'd had growing up.

With a look of dismay Dillon realized that almost every table was full. Boisterous families sat at large round tables catching up on the day's events. Lovers held hands across the smaller square tables, and a group of lanky teenagers dropped quarters into the video machines.

A smile tugged at the corner of his mouth as he

noticed his new neighbor . . . still husbandless. Walking over to where his sons were holding a discussion with Aaron on pizza, he smiled down at Elizabeth. "Hi. Fancy meeting you here."

"Hi. You picked a crowded night to visit Mario's."

"Is the food as good as it smells?"

Elizabeth noticed the hopeful gleam in his green eyes and chuckled. "Better. I recommend the spaghetti or the lasagna or the rigatoni. Then again the pizza is out of this world."

"Oh, great, major decision time."

"Dad, can we sit with Aaron?"

Looking into her son's hopeful eyes, Elizabeth shrugged her shoulders. "Please. Why don't you and your boys join us. We haven't ordered yet, and there does seem to be a shortage of tables."

"If you're sure it's no problem." Silently he could think of a very large problem: her husband decking him in a public restaurant for starters. He could see the headlines now: NEWCOMER FLATTENED IN MARIO'S. ARCHITECT TO HAVE ENTIRE MOUTH CAPPED."

As the boys scrambled to make room for each other on one seat, Dillon carefully slid in next to Elizabeth.

Elizabeth squashed herself up against the wall and took one whiff of his aftershave. Her mouth started to water. How had he managed to smell better than lasagna? How could she have forgotten how tall he was? He stood over six feet and had the muscular build of a linebacker. His shoulders looked as if they could carry the world, and they stretched the fabric of his emerald-green polo shirt. His clean faded jeans molded to his muscular thighs, and faded red sneakers completed his outfit.

His reddish-brown hair was cut and styled on the longish side, and his deep green eyes always seemed to be sparkling with either friendliness or insanity; at this point she wasn't placing any bets. His generous mouth had a natural upward slope and his voice was low and powerful.

"Elizabeth, Aaron, you have company tonight. No?"

Elizabeth smiled at Rosa, Mario's wife. "Not really. These are our new neighbors, Dillon McKenzie and his sons, Kevin and Kyle. They moved into Dr. Snyder's house today."

"Welcome, welcome. What a beautiful house. It's big, no? Only two babies to fill all those rooms? Where's their mother? You didn't leave her home? No? Ah, these poor babies have no mama. You must fill that house with many babies, but get a wife first." Taking a deep breath that emphasized her ample girth, she said, "I'll get water and a menu. No wife. Tsk, tsk. Don't worry. You come to Mario's, we take good care of you and the boys. They're too skinny, but don't worry. We'll fatten them up." Rosa left after depositing more menus on the table.

One look at Dillon's astonished face and Elizabeth burst out laughing. Her sweet laughter penetrated his shocked brain. "But—but I didn't get to say anything."

"I'm sorry, Dillon. I should have warned you about Rosa. She tends to mother the whole town. And the town lets her."

"Oh. What did she mean by my boys being skinny. They're not skinny, are they?"

She looked over the table at Kevin and Kyle and smiled. No, they weren't skinny. In fact they seemed to take after their father in build. Kyle and Aaron were the same age, yet Kyle was at least three inches taller and ten pounds heavier. Maybe it was Aaron who needed to be fattened up, although in school he seemed to be the same size as all the other kids. He wasn't the tallest in his class, but he wasn't the shortest either. "No, Dillon, they're not skinny. It's just Rosa's way. If someone isn't a doctor's cholesterol nightmare, they must not be eating right."

Satisfied with her answer he turned his attention to her appearance. She had replaced the foam-streaked jeans with trim khaki slacks, topped with a red short-sleeve sweater. Her dark hair was still pulled back in its braid, and he could detect a small amount of makeup.

In her large, deep brown eyes he saw intelligence, laughter, and uneasiness. Her high cheekbones accented her ordinary nose and sensational lips. He watched as small white teeth sank into those sensational lips and saw uncertainty enter her eyes. Taking a deep breath he asked the question that had been on his mind all day. "So where's Mr. Lancaster?"

"Long gone."

A feeling that felt too much like gladness flowed through his body. "How long?"

"Almost eight years."

Dillon did some quick arithmetic as he looked at her and Aaron. Elizabeth then heard his barely audible curse. Deciding a change in topic was called for, she said, "Look, here comes your water."

Dillon took the hint and allowed her to drop the subject, for now. A discussion followed about which of the dinners was the best. Elizabeth settled for lasagna, all the boys had pizza, and Dillon picked veal parmesan with spaghetti.

Dinner was a noisy affair with the three boys debating what to do the next day. Kevin offered to loan Aaron a skateboard while Kyle wanted to play army. Neither wanted to do Aaron's favorite pastime: reading or drawing.

With a frown Elizabeth realized how boring Aaron sounded for a seven-year-old boy. School hadn't been out a week, and all he wanted to do was read. Yuk! Didn't little boys like to go fishing? How about camping or baseball games with hotdogs and pretzels? For the first time she realized that being a good mother just might not be enough.

Dillon noticed the preoccupied expression Elizabeth wore as she stared at her son. Aaron was such a welcome change from his own sons. His boys were vocal, adventurous, and tended to get into trouble, while Aaron seemed quiet and intelligent. Maybe what his sons needed was the calming, gentle understanding of a mother. For the first time he realized that being a good father just might not be enough.

Elizabeth turned off the eleven-o'clock news with a disgusted sigh. How could people stand to watch it every night? Violence, death, and destruction, along with nuclear warheads, meltdowns, and the pending recession seemed to be the only headlines. As she turned off the lights and locked up, she saw that the lights were still on at Dillon's house. She slid in between the cool sheets and imagined him unloading boxes in his kitchen. If the number of boxes she had seen in the living room that afternoon was any indication, Dillon should be busy for the next year or so.

A soft smile curved her mouth as she thought about Dillon paying for their dinner. With a chuckle she realized it was the first time in eight years that a male had bought her dinner, and this time it was only because his dog had eaten her pansies. With the money she had saved, she was going to buy Aaron a fishing pole. Every boy should go fishing at least once in his life.

She sent a silent thank-you heavenward for sending Dillon and his sons to show her what Aaron might be missing. No one was ever going to call her son boring. His mother might be content to watch the world go by, but Aaron was going to join it. As sleep overtook her, a last lingering thought filtered through her brain. Starting tomorrow she was going to be a better dad.

With a sudden jerk Elizabeth sat up in bed and stared at the glowing red numbers on her clock: 2:20. What in the world had woken her up? She cautiously glanced around the room. Nothing seemed out of place. Swinging her legs over the side of the bed, she reached for her robe. It must be Aaron.

One arm was through the garment's sleeve when, looking out her bedroom window, she noticed the sporadic play of a flashlight's beam across the neighbor's lawn. Burglars? As sleep disappeared from her eyes she saw Dillon carrying something over by the old clothesline. Oh, Lord, no matter how attractive he was, he was crazy. Sneaking around in the dark with a mysterious package.

She stared, fascinated, as Dillon stuck the flashlight under his chin and lowered his burden to the ground. Then he reached down lithely and pulled up a towel. With a snap of his wrist he draped the bath towel over the line. A giggle escaped her mouth before she clamped a hand across it. *He was hanging laundry.* After buttoning up her robe she slipped quietly out her back door.

Dillon felt her presence before his eyes could focus on the ghostlike woman crossing the yard. She was wearing a lightweight robe that ended below her knees, and her dark hair was flowing down her back. A smile broke his face, the first in hours, as she held out a bag of clothespins to him. "Thanks," he said.

Together they began hanging the sheets and towels as best they could with one faint beam of light. After pinning a row of washcloths, Dillon asked, "You're not going to ask?"

With laughter barely contained in her voice, she replied, "You're not going to tell me?"

"Oh, hell. Where do you want me to start?"

"The beginning is always a good place."

Dillon grabbed a queen-size sheet and began. "You already know about the dog bath." He detected a faint chuckle but continued, "What you didn't know was the boys overflowed the tub, and I dumped the entire box of towels on the floor to soak up the water."

She bent down to get another towel. "Logical."

"I promised the boys pizza after we all took showers. There wasn't a clean towel in the house so we dried off with sheets." He handed the flashlight to Elizabeth. "After we got home tonight I went into the basement and threw the first load into the washer. I knew I should have stayed in the basement while the first load washed, considering the machine hadn't been used in two years. But everything seemed to be working and the boys needed sheets on their beds for the night."

Elizabeth played the beam of light across the line and followed his every movement as he clipped the sheet to the clothesline.

"While I was upstairs the water hose cracked. I guess it was dry rotted. There was water all over the basement by the time I went back down. After I repaired the hose it worked fine. By the time the first load was finished I realized there wasn't a dryer. So I washed three more loads, and here I am, hanging laundry in the middle of the night."

She chuckled softly. "It wasn't as bad as I feared."

"The water hose?"

"No, the reason you were prowling around outside after the witching hour."

He hung the last towel. "I guess we seem kind

of crazy. Every time you come around I'm doing something out of the ordinary."

"That's true. But the jury's still out if you're crazy or not." As she reached for the remaining clothespins, she handed Dillon back the flashlight. "Good night."

Dillon reached for the flashlight and accidentally grabbed her wrist. Heat spread through his fingers as a warm feeling settled in his stomach. "Elizabeth?"

Her startled gaze flew to his.

His husky "I'll be crazy if I don't do this" was whispered the moment before his lips captured hers.

Three

Warmth spread through her entire body as she closed her eyes and surrendered to Dillon's kiss. With a gentle coaxing of his tongue he entered the sweet haven of her mouth.

A shudder slid down his spine and a groan vibrated deep in his throat as Elizabeth slowly opened her lips. She raised her soft hands to caress his neck as her full womanly breasts pressed against his heart.

Strong arms pulled her closer to his heated body as cool moist grass cushioned her bare feet. Contrasts, everything was in contrasts: the warmth of his mouth, the coolness of the night, the softness of her breast against the hardness of his chest. The mere size of Dillon suggested strength and power, while the touch of his lips was gently seductive.

Dillon felt desire shoot through his body. When arousal stirred thick and hard he released a groan. With reluctance he broke the kiss and trailed a path down her neck till he reached the barrier of her robe. At first he only meant to kiss her, to taste her lips. He meant the kiss to be friendly, a nice neighborly kiss. Hell, who was he kidding? Neighbors didn't go around kissing each other.

When Elizabeth responded so sweetly, desire blazed through him like an inferno. Passion wasn't what he'd expected when he kissed her. Sweet Lord, she was his neighbor; he planned on raising his boys in this house. How in the hell was he to do that with this delicious piece of temptation living next door? He placed one last kiss on the corner of her mouth and released her. Elizabeth felt him move away and slowly opened her eyes. Oh Lord, that wasn't a kiss; that was heaven. Liquid heat had settled in the pit of her stomach, and an empty feeling filled her inner core.

Oh, sweet Mary, what had she done? Fiery red rushed up her cheeks as she hastily stepped backward. An inner voice screamed that she should run home and lock the door. Her sensible side told her to act like kissing a man at two-thirty in the morning after hanging laundry wasn't anything out of the ordinary.

Thankful that the darkness hid her blush, she whispered, "Good night."

Dillon watched the whiteness of her robe disappear into the darkness. For the first time in his adult life he felt like throwing a temper tantrum. Why hadn't he checked up on his neighbors before buying his dream house? What he didn't need was a sweet, gentle woman living next door to show him just what he was missing. With a last glance toward her neat and orderly house, he walked through his back door into chaos.

Four hours of sleep and three cups of coffee later he still wasn't ready to face the morning. Why couldn't the birds sing more quietly or the newspaper boy oil his bicycle chain? At six-thirty he had heard the bike three streets away. Now it wasn't quite eight and the boys still weren't up.

Standing by the front screen door drinking his coffee, he watched the neighborhood come awake. Directly across the street an elderly couple came out of their house decked out in their Sunday best. The man wore a sky-blue leisure suit, that looked amazingly dashing on someone seventy years old. The woman was dressed in fluorescent yellow and lime green with a wide brim hat to match. A smile formed on Dillon's lips as he watched what was obviously a weekly ritual. The woman waited by the driveway as the old man went out back to the garage. A whistle escaped his lips as he saw a white-and-red Edsel in mint condition back down the driveway.

As the couple drove away they beeped and waved to someone. With a quick turn of his head he saw Elizabeth and Aaron head down the sidewalk toward town. She was dressed in a bright floral-print skirt with a fushia sleeveless sweater to match. Her hair was in its usual braid that swung saucily with every step. Aaron could have posed for a Normal Rockwell picture. He was dressed in black pants and a short-sleeve white dress shirt with his hair still wet from trying to control a stubborn cowlick.

He watched as they walked away. His smile died as he tried to remember when he and his sons had last gone to church.

With a yawn he stretched and tried to work out some of the kinks that had settled in his back from sleeping on the sofa. After Elizabeth had disappeared the night before, he had gone into the kitchen and started to unload boxes. He was glad he had paid a cleaning service to come in and clean the entire house the day before he'd moved in. The number of cabinets in the kitchen alone was astounding.

When he'd first been married, he and Rachael

had owned a condominium in a nice section of Philadelphia. Their dream was owning a house in the country, but something always came up that was more important. Two years ago a car accident had taken his wife, and all those things that had come up suddenly didn't matter.

For two years he'd struggled with the loss of his wife and single parenthood. Neither had been easy. Accepting his wife's death had been easier than living with the regret. He had married his college sweetheart the year after they graduated. Both had been career minded, and there was harmony in their marriage. Four years later Rachael had gotten pregnant with Kevin. They had decided that Rachael should postpone her career to raise the baby while Dillon continued full speed ahead with his. Two promotions later Rachael had gotten pregnant with Kyle, and discontentment settled in.

Rachael was left in a condominium to raise two active boys while he worked twelve to fourteen hours a day. By then he was in partnership with a prestigious architecture firm in the center of the city, and a house in the country wasn't feasible. Three days before Kyle was to start kindergarten and day care, Rachael, on her way home from an employment agency, got caught in a ten-car pileup on the Schuylkill Expressway. There were six fatalities; Rachael was one.

Dillon was left with a demanding job, two small, confused boys who looked at him as if he were a stranger, and a deep feeling of regret. How could he possibly have been so selfish? What had happened to all his dreams of a family? He had had one right under his nose and never noticed it; he had been too busy climbing the ladder to a better position. Months after the funeral, he had stood in the rain at Rachael's grave and begged for forgiveness. A sense of tranquility had come over him, and, for the first time in months, he felt he could make it. The next morning he had set the wheels of a new life into motion.

It was a slow process, but he had begun to live every day to its fullest. He'd become a father to his sons. He'd branched out on his own from the firm. A year later he'd found his dream house. He was financially able to support his family, and there wasn't one regret, until now.

Shaking his head he wasn't sure if he regretted kissing Elizabeth or regretted not asking her to stay. The sound of shouting from upstairs brought him out of his reverie.

"Give me that."

"No, it's mine, you turkey."

"Daaaaad!"

Placing his empty cup on a stack of boxes marked MISCELLANEOUS, he understood now why their old neighbors had thrown a going-away party when they moved. A lot could be said for peace and quiet. Stretching his arms above his head, he prepared to start his day. First thing on the list was setting up his bed and putting dry sheets on it.

"Dad, Kevin's stealing my underwear."

"That's because Dad threw all mine away."

With an exasperated sigh Dillon started up the stairs. "Kevin, why would I throw away your underwear?"

"Because you love Kyle more than me."

Dillon came to a halt in the upstairs hall. He knew the next words out of Kevin's mouth would be something like, "you bought Kyle this." In the past two years guilt and compassion had worn down his firmness with his sons. Staring at the open door to Kevin's bedroom, he admitted that maybe Kevin and Kyle were spoiled. Was it possible to overcompensate on love?

As he entered the room he tripped over a football. He looked around, and for the first time really noticed the ridiculous number of toys. Balls of every shape and size overflowed from opened boxes; baseball bats were scattered about. Boxes filled with G.I. Joes and mutant aliens blocked the way to the closet. Ice skates, roller skates, and a pair of spikes hung by their laces from doorknobs, while Boris, the pet hamster, merrily ran around in circles in his cage.

With a disgusted sigh Dillon knew Kyle's room would look exactly the same, except for the hamster. Kyle had an ant farm. Maybe it was time for dad to learn to say no.

Elizabeth closed the oven door and pushed a stray piece of hair out of her eyes. The soft summer breeze coming in the windows did little to cool down the heat in the kitchen. With the oven on for the past two hours and a pot of chicken soup bubbling away, it was a useless battle. The heat always won. Summer was the worst time to be in her business, but it paid the bills.

Leaning against the counter, she took a drink of ice-cold lemonade and closed her eyes. Two cakes were cooling, and the third one was in the oven. Tonight after dinner she'd decorate them, and when the sun went down she'd bake a couple of batches of cookies. From outside she heard the voices of the boys next door. Aaron had been so anxious to have them come over and play that he barely ate lunch.

With an amused smile she thought about all the different kinds of things Aaron could do with his new playmates. The smile slowly faded when her thoughts shifted to their father. What in the world ever possessed her to go out to help him last night? She should have stayed inside and pretended she didn't see him. That's what a sensible, dull person would have done. And wasn't she supposed to be boring? What would she say to him the next time they met? She wondered if he'd believe she walked in her sleep.

The phone rang just as a knock sounded on her back screen door. Seeing Kyle through the screen, she called, "Come on in, boys." Turning her back, she reached for the phone on the kitchen wall. "Hello?"

Dillon's mouth watered as he followed his sons in the back door. One look at Elizabeth and he wasn't sure what caused that reaction: her shorts or the delicious aroma that filled the kitchen. With her back toward them he listened to her talk about cakes while flipping through a calendar. He watched as she wrote down what appeared to be an order.

Tearing his eyes away from her, he scanned the yellow-and-blue kitchen. There were bowls piled high in the sink, layers of cake sat on the counter cooling, and a fat white cat was curled up on a wooden chair. With a frown he realized there wasn't a dishwasher or a microwave in sight. Elizabeth Lancaster was truly an old-fashioned cook.

Dillon walked over to the kitchen table and picked up one of the business cards lying on top of unfolded baker's boxes. The card read INDE-SCRIBABLY DELICIOUS in bold black letters; in smaller print was Elizabeth's name and phone number. If the German chocolate cake he'd tasted last night was a sample of her cooking, Betty Crocker didn't stand a chance. Dillon pocketed one of the cards.

Elizabeth hung up the phone and turned around. She kept her eyes on the boys, not trusting herself to meet his gaze. "Aaron's in his room. Why don't you go get him."

She watched as the boys hurried from the room. Then she headed for a safe harbor, the pile of dirty dishes. "Thanks for letting them come over and play. They'll be just fine. You can head on back. I'm sure you have lots to do." Grabbing the bottle of dish lotion she squirted too much in the sink and groaned. Had she really just ordered the poor man out of her house?

Dillon saw bubbles fill the white porcelain sink and grinned. She wasn't as calm as she appeared. "Is it all right if Kevin and Kyle stay here while I go food shopping?" he asked. "Old Mother Hubbard's cupboards are bare."

"Sure. That's what neighbors are for."

He watched as she practically scrubbed the finish off a bowl, then rinsed it. "As soon as I get back, I'll take Aaron over to my house and give you a break."

The echo of her "Fine" followed him out the screen door. Cutting across the lawn he took a deep breath and headed toward his van. Sweat broke out across his brow when he thought about the kiss they'd shared the evening before. Maybe the aroma of detergent was beginning to affect his libido? How could a person remember every minute detail, every texture, every smell and the sound she made when their tongues first mated. With a muffled curse he climbed into his vehicle and jammed the key into the ignition. He turned the air conditioner on full blast in an attempt to cool down before he met the cashiers at the local grocery store.

An hour and a half later Elizabeth sat on her porch laughing. Dillon was standing awkwardly on a skateboard trying to teach Aaron how to use it, without much success. Kevin and Kyle expertly sailed down the driveway, performing sharp right turns and wheelies on the sidewalk.

Two falls later Dillon was still trying. Elizabeth clamped a hand across her mouth to muffle the laugh that escaped her lips as Dillon almost lost his balance again.

Safely bringing his skateboard to a halt, Dillon glared at the woman giggling at his expense. She was sitting in the shade of her porch with her feet up on the railing. Ten minutes earlier she had been engrossed in a book; now she seemed more amused by the sight of him making a total idiot of himself. What did she expect? He wasn't a young man anymore. Bracing his hands on his hips, he yelled across the yard, "At least I'm trying."

Elizabeth stopped laughing. He was right. Here she sat like a piece of dead wood while he tried to teach her son how to ride a skateboard. Where were the rules that said a mother couldn't teach a child to skateboard? Was she so dull that she couldn't fit her body on a four-inch-wide board and roll down a hill? Visions of multiple contusions flitted across her brain. Well, maybe she should start with something less physical.

Like fishing. Fishing was a nice quiet relaxing sport. A lot of fathers went fishing. How hard could it be to sit in a folding chair, watch a red-and-white bobber, and down a six-pack of beer. Okay, scratch the beer and substitute fruit juice. If she was going to raise Aaron properly, she had to start acting like a father too. Maybe she could convince Aaron to bait the hooks.

With a frown she watched as Dillon patiently explained to Kyle how shifting his body weight caused the board to turn, not the movement of his feet. Aaron seemed to be hanging on his every word. Having Dillon move in next door was a stroke of luck. She could watch him with his sons and take lessons on how to be a father.

Dillon answered Kyle's question and glanced back in time to see her disappear into the house. He hoped she realized that he'd just been teasing about trying. With the sun shining in his eyes, he wasn't positive, but he thought he'd seen her frown. Telling the boys to behave, he followed Elizabeth inside. He found her in the kitchen placing cups on a tray already loaded with cookies. "Elizabeth?"

She looked up from arranging the cups. "Dillon?"

Nervously shifting his weight, he wondered how to go about explaining something unexplainable. When he saw her go inside, something told him to follow. He feared that somehow he had hurt her.

Elizabeth noticed his mussed-up hair and remembered how soft it felt when she had run her fingers through it. A blush swept up her cheek as she remembered how warm his lips had been and how strong his arms had felt.

When she returned to her bed last night a strange feeling of contentment had followed her into sleep. During her shower this morning she'd lectured herself on things that could never be. Dillon was as different from her as horses were from camels. Horses raced, jumped, or otherwise galloped through life. Camels slowly plodded a steady course. No one ever wanted to own a camel, but sometimes they were necessary. But what would a Thoroughbred want with a camel?

Dillon saw a touch of pink stain her cheeks. Disappointment raced through him as he watched her lips frown. "Elizabeth?"

She heard the question in his voice and ran her tongue over suddenly dry lips. The part of her that responded to his kiss screamed for a replay, while the sensible side asked for the only thing she could ever have from Dillon. "Would you please teach me to be a father?"

Four

"A father?" Running fingers through his hair, Dillon stared at Elizabeth. This delectable, soft-spoken, intelligent woman wanted to be a *father*? Shaking his head hoping to unclog his hearing, he repeated, "A father?"

"You know, a father. Someone who takes his son fishing and to ball games. I'm okay with base-ball, but football has me totally confused. I know there are field goals, downs, and foul shots."

"Foul shots are in basketball."

A huge grin split her face. "See, a real father knows that kind of stuff. One day Aaron will be asking me questions that I wouldn't know how to answer."

The dazzling smile that lit up her face caused a spark to light deep within him. How could she have remained so fresh and innocent in this day and age? Raising a child alone was a tough job, he knew. "Elizabeth, they didn't give me any in-structions on fatherhood the day Kevin was born. It's a hit or miss situation. Just use your com-mon sense."

Her smile crumbled. "You won't teach me?"

"I didn't say that." With an exasperated sigh, he said, "Where did you want to start? We could go over to my place, guzzle a couple of six-packs of beer while we watch a baseball game."

She giggled. "That's not exactly what I had in mind."

"I could teach you how to belch." Hearing her chuckle turn into a laugh, he smiled. "How about parallel parking?" Watching her dark chocolate eyes fill with laughter caused a riot of emotions to rush through his body. With a gentle hand he reached out and tenderly brushed a damp tendril of hair off her forehead. Laughter faded into awareness as the heat in the kitchen became stifling.

Elizabeth looked up into his suddenly serious green eyes and almost forgot how to breathe. This was the Dillon who'd kissed her under the clothesline and awakened a secret desire buried deep within her. She should concentrate on the task at hand, she told herself. She knew she was a darn good mother. Dillon had almost agreed to help her become a better father, but maybe what she wanted was for him to teach her to become a woman?

Breaking eye contact she scolded herself for that last thought. She was perfectly happy with her life; she only needed help in the father category. The woman part didn't fit in. Dillon was her next-door neighbor, would remain a neighbor for years to come, and would hopefully become a friend. Staring down at the tray of empty glasses, she headed for the refrigerator for the pitcher of lemonade.

As she filled the glasses she informed him, "I already know how to parallel park."

"Really?" Dillon raised an eyebrow. "So what did you have in mind?"

"Fishing."

Seeing his frown she continued, "I realize you must have a million things to do with having just moved in and with your job. But how about if your next free day we all go fishing? There's a really nice spot just outside of town. I see people fishing there all the time."

"How's tomorrow?"

"Tomorrow? I didn't mean to rush you, Dillon. Just whenever you do something fatherly with Kyle and Kevin, maybe Aaron and I could tag along. You know, pick up some pointers."

Hearing the hopeful note in her voice, he would have promised her anything. "I've given myself a vacation for the next two weeks. After that I'll be working at home."

"But we haven't worked out what you get in return."

He thought of some possibilities, but they weren't very fatherly. Trying to lighten up the mood before his libido got totally out of control, he asked with a comical leer, "What did you have in mind?"

She saw his teasing smile and it eased some of her tension. She really should be ashamed of herself thinking he'd ask for something totally inappropriate. Here he was being a good neighbor and friend while she was carrying around indecent thoughts. "Are you going to work this summer with the boys home?"

"Sure."

"Oh." A note of concern crept into her voice. "Have you ever worked while the boys were home all day?"

"I've been working out of my house for the past six months."

"Yeah, but Kevin and Kyle were in school."

With renewed insight he realized that having

the boys underfoot all day might present a problem. "Bad move, huh?"

"I'll make you a deal. When I take Aaron to the local pool, Kevin and Kyle can tag along. That should give you a couple of peaceful hours. In exchange you will give me fatherhood lessons when you get a chance."

"Somehow I think you got the short end of the stick on that deal." With a smile he held out his hand. "I'll think of some way to even up the ante. Let's shake on it, and tomorrow I'll teach you how to fish."

Elizabeth felt her small hand being swallowed up by his large, strong one, and a shiver slid down her spine. How could the mere feel of his hand have such an impact on her? She pulled her mind off the heat radiating from his hand and asked, "I don't have to use worms do I?"

Releasing her soft trembling hand, Dillon wasn't sure if he was the cause of the tremble or if the thought of baiting the hook was. "No, you don't have to use worms, even if they're the best bait. You can make dough balls."

"Dough balls?"

"You take bread and wet it with water. Then you roll little balls that fit on the hook."

"Plain bread?" At his nod she made a face. "That doesn't sound very appetizing."

"Worms don't appeal to me either, but trout love them." He laughed.

Elizabeth listened to his rich laughter, and happiness filled her heart. She'd found a friend. "How about if we go around eleven and I'll pack a picnic lunch for us?"

"Okay, you bring the food and I'll bring the drinks and the worms. Deal?" He lifted the tray of drinks and cookies and headed for the front porch. The screen door slammed, followed by Dillon's bellow, "Come on boys, break time."

• • •

With a quick yawn and a hugh stretch, Dillon looked out the den window into the night. Somewhere nearby an owl hooted at the moon and crickets were having a field day. It was after one o'clock, and Elizabeth was still up. Lights were still blazing in her kitchen and living room. Maybe he should go over and check on her, or maybe he should stay home and mind his own business.

He looked back at the old room that had been the doctor's examining room. Three solid-oak file cabinets stood sentry along one wall while French doors leading to a back patio were opened to let in the cool evening breeze. Built-in bookshelves lined each side of the fireplace, where blackened brick testified to evenings spent reading in front of a blazing fire. Muddy-green walls were marked with brighter green squares, where diplomas and certificates once hung.

Tomorrow morning he would go into town to buy green paint, not the original dark green but something soothing and homey. Since this was the room he would be using as an office, it was going to be the first one renovated. As soon as he got it painted he could get all the office furniture out of the living room and dining room.

He looked out the side window again. The lights were still on. Would she mind if he went over? What excuse could he make? What was the proper, neighborly thing to do? Hell, how was he supposed to know? For over a dozen years he had lived in a condo, where everyone minded their own business.

If she looks at me as if I were crazy, I'll ask to borrow a cup of sugar or something. He had taken five steps when the lights in her kitchen turned off. A moment later the living room light met the same fate. At least he'd been saved from making a total fool of himself. Standing in the darkness he watched the house settle in for the night and silently wished Elizabeth sweet dreams.

Elizabeth and Aaron made the last delivery and headed back home in the car. In the back seat two new fishing poles were lying across the seat along with a tackle box. Hiding a yawn behind her hand, she turned into her driveway and spotted Kevin and Kyle waiting for them.

"Where were you? We thought you were going to be late."

Slowly climbing out of the car she smiled at the anxious boys. "You didn't really think we'd miss this trip did you?"

"Fishing's okay, I guess." Kevin looked thoughtful for a moment, then smiled. "Dad said you're packing a picnic lunch."

Elizabeth opened the back door of her Ford Escort and reached in for her purchases. "Yes, I'm bringing the food." Silently she congratulated herself on making enough to feed an army. She had seen how much pizza they had eaten Saturday night.

"Great. See Kyle, I told you Mrs. Lancaster wouldn't let us starve."

"Didn't you boys eat breakfast?"

"Just cereal. Dad can't cook."

"At all?" Elizabeth asked.

"He's not too bad with the microwave," Kevin said. "But radioactive pancakes get boring after a while."

She suppressed a shudder. "Aaron, why don't you go play with Kevin and Kyle while I finish packing our lunch."

A half hour later Elizabeth was sitting on her grandmother's old quilt under a weeping willow whose branches stretched across a small creek.

Dillon sat next to her with a bandage on his thumb, silently cursing the manufacturer of Aaron's fishing pole. Who would have thought putting together a plastic rod could be so complicated? he wondered, recalling the pain of dislodging a hook from his finger. "Aaron, come get your rod."

Aaron looked at his brand new, shiny red fishing rod and beamed. "Thank you, Mr. McKenzie, for putting it together for me." He bent over and kissed his mother's cheek. "Thanks, Mom."

"You're welcome, honey. That's a present for doing so well in school. Maybe next year it'll be a new bike." Watching her son's eyes widen, she smiled. "Why don't you go on back to Kevin and Kyle. I'm sure they will teach you how to hook a worm."

Dillon chuckled. "That's 'bait the hook.' "

Elizabeth turned her head and studied Dillon. He was dressed in faded cutoffs and a blue T-shirt that was stretched to its limits. With the sun beating down, his hair glowed with red highlights. Sitting this close to Dillon on a soft hand-stitched quilt that had once covered a bed wasn't such a good idea. There was something too intimate about it.

With a nervous gesture she grabbed the second package and handed it to Dillon. "You have to put mine together too, or no lunch."

An eyebrow shot up. "What's in the basket?"

"Will the answer have anything to do with the condition of my pole?"

"Wrong answer, and I guarantee you won't be able to reel in any fish that nibbles on your dough balls."

Elizabeth smiled in satisfaction. "I'll have you know I made the best dough balls east of the Mississippi." When Dillon continued to stare skeptically at the large wicker basket, she added, "Okay, let me see. There's a choice between chicken salad sandwiches or roast beef on rye. There's also potato salad, macaroni salad, deviled eggs, pickles, fresh vegetables, and dip. I packed some potato chips and pretzels, and I made a cherry cheese cake."

"All that in one basket?"

"The miracle of stackable Tupperware."

Dillon's stomach reminded him of two hastily drunk cups of coffee and the bowl of cereal the boys swore tasted just like chocolate chip cookies. It hadn't.

Seeing the hungry look on his face made Elizabeth laugh. "You better put mine together faster than Aaron's or the cherry cheese cake will go bad."

With renewed vigor Dillon tore into the plastic-wrapped package with a dark comment. With sure fingers he secured the three pole sections together and started to thread the line through the eyes. "So tell me, Elizabeth Lancaster, what did you ever do that was so good to deserve a boy like Aaron?"

Caught off guard by his serious question, she asked, "What do you mean, a boy like Aaron?"

"He's obedient, polite, and very well mannered."

A frown crossed her face. "You could be describing a well-trained dog."

Dillon's fingers froze on the latch to the tackle box. There was pain in her voice. He studied the lovely woman sitting crossed-legged in front of him. Her head was bent and she was idly tracing the design on the faded quilt. Her long, dark brown hair was pulled back into a braid, held together by a pink rubberband.

With a gentle gesture he raised her chin and looked into the saddest brown eyes he had ever seen. "What's wrong with Aaron?" He watched perfect white teeth sink into her lower trembling lip and grimace. He would bet the next mortgage payment that she was desperately holding back tears. Fear raced through him as images of all the possible things that could be wrong with Aaron flashed through his mind. "Elizabeth, what's wrong with Aaron?"

"He's too good."

Dillon blinked. "Too good?" When she nodded he asked, "At what?"

"Everything. Do you know he just got straight A's on his report card?" When Dillon stared at her as if she had sprouted another head, her voice rose another notch. "His first word wasn't 'mommy,' it was 'please.' He has never forgotten to say please or thank you. He has never been spanked or sent to his room. Do you know he's in a third-grade reader and can actually do some multiplication?"

Noticing the stupid grin spreading across Dillon's face, she raised her voice. "He's not a normal boy. Since the day he was toilet trained, he never once forgot to put the seat back down on the toilet. How would you like to have the only boy in Pennsylvania who never once used his sleeve for a napkin or a tissue?"

Dillon really tried not to, but he burst out laughing. She was *complaining* because her son could be nominated to sainthood, all he needed was three miracles and he'd be a shoo-in.

"Go ahead and laugh, Dillon. You have two perfectly normal boys. I bet you don't have any problems with them."

"Problems? I'll have you know that Kevin barely passed third grade and Kyle still has a tendency to write letters backward. My boys never learned to say a simple please or thank-you, no matter how many times I remind them. With three males in the house, our toilet seat is never down. And if tissue companies depended on my boys for a profit, the company would have folded years ago."

"Oh."

"Yeah, oh. Do you want to trade?"

"No. It's just sometimes I worry about Aaron. He's not a genius or anything. It's just that his favorite pastime is reading. He doesn't seem to want to do normal stuff."

"Hence, the fatherhood lessons?"

"Aaron was only two when his grandfather passed away. So he hadn't had any male influences in his life. I want him to have a more rounded childhood."

Dillon hated to voice the next question. "What about his real father?"

Elizabeth glanced over and smiled at the three boys fishing in the distance. "When I was three months pregnant my husband informed me that he wanted a divorce. It seemed he wasn't ready to settle down with a wife and baby. The agreement was that he would never contact the child or me." She'd given him the abridged version; she saw no real reason to tell Dillon about the sexy young blonde that had hung on her husband's arm when he delivered that speech.

Dillon realized her story had some gaping holes big enough for the Titanic to fall into. "What about support?"

"Support?"

"Child support. Weekly checks or something."

"That was in the agreement. No support, no visitation rights. I made sure Ron would never have a claim on Aaron."

He swore vehemently. "What kind of lawyer did you have?"

Elizabeth was startled by the anger behind his

words. She laid a gentle hand on top of his tightly clinched fist. "Dillon, it doesn't matter. I got what I wanted. I've seen children who weren't wanted. That's not how I wanted my son to live. This agreement suited us both."

Dillon still could not believe that a father could disown his own flesh and blood. "Didn't he ever try to contact you?"

"No. He never even inquired if he had a son or a daughter."

He cursed again.

A gentle smile touched Elizabeth's lips. "Would you really want to see Aaron go off every other weekend with someone like that?"

Unclenching his fist, he gently held her hand. "No, I guess you're right. But he should have been made to take financial responsibility for the life he created."

"If I'd let him do that, he would have the right to make decisions about Aaron's life." With one last gentle smile she changed the subject. "You better hurry up with my pole. I think the boys are losing patience with the fish."

Dillon watched as Kevin and Kyle reeled in their lines. Aaron stood perfectly still and watched his bobber. Dillon smiled. One more thing Aaron was good at: patience. With sure fingers Dillon finished his task by attaching a hook, sinkers, and a flashy bobber to Elizabeth's pole.

When she saw that her pole was almost ready, Elizabeth reached into the picnic basket and pulled out a small raspberry-colored container. She selected one of the small balls inside and gently slid it on the hook.

"What in the world are they?"

"They're dough balls."

"I have never seen dough balls like that. What did you do to them?"

Elizabeth looked back at her container with satisfaction. Three dozen assorted flavors of dough balls sat in precise lines according to flavor. She knew that if she were a fish, plain, white bread would sound unappealing. So she'd divided the balls into six groups of six, rolling the first group in cracker meal, the next group in corn meal, and the others in parsley, parmesan cheese, and paprika. The last six balls she left plain, just to satisfy Dillon. "I figure the fish would like a nice change of pace."

Dillon looked at her hopeful expression and kept his mouth shut. If she thought she could catch trout with paprika, who was he to argue. "Come on. I'll show you how to cast."

She took her pole and walked the few feet to the edge of the stream and waved to the boys. A breathless "oh" escaped her lips as Dillon stood behind her and wrapped his arms around her to hold the rod.

"When you want to release the line you push this button, and when you're ready to reel in the line you turn this crank." Dillon knew he shouldn't be standing so close to her, but he could not resist. Her head was bent trying to concentrate on the reel. Her long, dark hair smelled like honeysuckle, and his arms ached from wanting to pull her into them.

Elizabeth felt the heat of Dillon's arms around her, and she longed to sink deeper into the safety of his embrace. She wasn't sure his arms offered safety. The longer she stood like this, the more dangerous it seemed. She watched his strong fingers gently hold the rod and wondered how they would feel softly caressing her skin.

Quickly turning her thoughts away from Dillon's hands and back to fishing, she said, "That looks easy enough. What's next?"

His mind raced with the possibilities. One step

closer and he would feel her body pressed against the entire length of his. She was so little in his arms, his chin could rest on top of her head. If she stood five feet four it was because she was wearing padded socks. His grandfather would have called her a wee lass, but since Dillon was born and raised in America, he thought of her as a delectable morsel. One that was, yes, indescribably delicious.

With a ruthless shake he ordered himself to concentrate on fishing lessons. This was Aaron's mother; she was also a neighbor and a friend. Most important, she was the woman who was going to take his sons to the pool so he could get some work done. She was going to receive the best daddy lessons he could devise.

"Next I'll show you how to cast." Trying to clear the huskiness from his voice, he said, "Put your hand here and get ready to push the button as you swing the pole."

Elizabeth followed his instructions. She pointed the rod behind her, and with Dillon's hands resting on top of hers she gently arched the pole straight up and over her shoulder while depressing the button.

It was a perfect cast. Hook, line, and sinker sailed gracefully twenty feet in the air.

It was a real shame the creek was only eight feet wide.

Elizabeth could feel the laugh Dillon was trying so gallantly to suppress. His chest was silently vibrating and there was a strange choking sound coming from his throat. With laughter shining in her eyes she leaned back and looked up at him. "Well, teach, how did I do?"

Having her so near was more than any man could stand. With a smile curving his sensual lips, he placed a quick kiss on a pair of unsuspecting ones. "Not bad at all for the first time. Are you sure you have never done this before?"

The short kiss surprised her, but she decided not to mention it. "Nope, I've never been fishing before. But wasn't the hook supposed to land in the water?"

Dillon gave this some serious thought. "You could have a point there."

Five

Elizabeth felt something tickling her nose and brushed her hand at the offending object. When the tickling sensation was repeated she mumbled something incoherent and swiped again. She was not going to open her eyes and get up. It was too peaceful.

"Rise and shine, Sleeping Beauty."

In the far recesses of her mind, Elizabeth smiled. Dreams were such wonderful things. Here she was dreaming her sexy new neighbor had called her Sleeping Beauty. A gentle breeze blew, and the sound of rustling leaves caused a frown to replace the smile. Why would leaves be rustling in her bedroom?

Dillon leaned on his elbow watching her. He wondered what delicious thoughts were going through her mind. When a frown replaced the smile he impulsively leaned down to kiss the pout away.

Elizabeth felt the warmth of the kiss and sighed, "Dillon."

With a groan he pulled her closer as she slid her arms around his neck and whispered his name.

Even in her sleep she knew who it was. His control was slipping fast with Elizabeth lying partly under him and responding so passionately.

Responding? She was dominating the kiss. He was trying to hold on to sanity, when she arched her back and pressed her breasts against his chest. In the back of his mind he knew the boys were exploring farther down the creek. He also knew he shouldn't be doing this, but, hell, he was human.

One hand slid up from her waist to gently cup her full breast just as his tongue slipped in between her teeth. A moan quivered in his throat when he felt Elizabeth freeze. With every ounce of control he possessed he broke the kiss, and pulled back. Her large sleep-laden eyes stared back at him. He wasn't sure if they held confusion or desire. Running his hand through his hair, he tried to bring his breathing back to normal. "Good morning, sleepy head."

Elizabeth stared at Dillon in total confusion. She suddenly realized where she was. Dillon had given her casting lessons, and with her rod propped up against a stick, she had called the boys to lunch. She'd never seen three males devour so much food at one sitting. Aaron looked slightly surprised, but he dug in while something was still left.

Later Dillon had taken the boys farther downstream to see if they would have better luck, and she had lain down in the shade of the weeping willow and watched her red-and-white bobber that never bobbed.

That was the last thing she remembered until Dillon's kiss. She must have fallen asleep. Great. She'd just slept through her first fatherhood lesson. That's what happened when she stayed up all night to bake cookies and cakes.

Embarrassment flared in her cheeks, and she dropped her eyes to Dillon's chest. Watching the rapid rise and fall of his light blue T-shirt was having a direct effect on her heart rate. But she knew he'd been affected too. Joy exploded in her heart. She, Elizabeth Lancaster, had caused this condition in sexy Dillon McKenzie. She really shouldn't be so proud of herself; it was a lousy condition to be in. But since she was in the same condition, it was wonderful.

What she knew about men could be written on a matchbook, but Dillon didn't seem the type to go around kissing just anyone.

Dillon watched the emotions that played over Elizabeth's lovely face. When she looked at him again, her eyes were troubled. "Where are the boys?"

He laid back on the quilt and threw his arm over his eyes. "They went farther downstream to explore." Half of him had expected her to slap his face for taking advantage of her while she was sleeping. The other half prayed for desire to be mirrored in those huge dark eyes. What he didn't expect was concern. Was she upset because he'd kissed her, or that she'd responded? Maybe she thought the boys were all standing around watching him attack Aaron's mother.

Elizabeth sat up and examined the body lying next to her. Power, strength, and pure maleness were the impressions she was forming when a movement out of the corner of her eye caught her attention. Her bobber was bobbing. "Dillon, I think I've got a nibble."

"What?" he choked out. "What do you want to nibble on?"

The bobber was moving violently now. "I don't have *to* nibble, I've got *a* nibble." She rose to her feet. "Hurry, Dillon. I think I've caught a fish."

He opened his eyes just as she bent over to pick up her pole. He watched her start to jump up and down in excitement. Lord knew how that was going to affect the fish.

Frantically she stared at the bobber as it disappeared beneath the water. "Dillon, what do I do?"

With a smile he leaned back on his elbows. "Reel him in."

"How?"

"Turn the crank on the rod." He watched in amusement. Excitement and concentration shone on her face as she battled wits against a trout. When he noticed her moving along the shore instead of bringing the fish in, he yelled, "Reel him in, Elizabeth."

"I'm trying." She came to a stop under a low-hanging branch of the weeping willow. "It won't turn, Dillon." Not waiting for help she yanked with all her might on the pole.

He watched astonished as sinker, bobber, and fish flew ten feet straight up and over her head, the line tangling itself in a branch. He stood with his hands on his hips staring up into the thick green leaves. Fifteen feet above the ground a twelve-inch-long trout wiggled its tail.

There was panic in Elizabeth's voice. "It's alive."

Chuckling, Dillon turned his attention back to her. "Of course it's alive now, but it won't be for long. Then you can take it home and cook it up." He watched as the color drained from her face. "Elizabeth?"

"Dillon, please don't let him die." Her fingers grasped his arm and squeezed. "Please save him."

Looking back up into the tree he saw the fish still wiggling. "Honey, that's what fishing is all about. You catch fish, bring them home, and eat them."

Her voice rose in panic. "If I wanted to eat fish, I'd go to a grocery store." Seeing Dillon's bewildered look, she added, "If you save my fish, I will cook a complete chicken dinner for you and the boys."

Grabbing the lower branch he swung himself up. "Fried or roasted?"

"Fried."

Pulling himself up on the next branch he shouted, "With mashed potatoes?"

Dillon was almost to the wiggling fish when she answered, "And gravy."

"Grab that net and stand under me. When the fish lands in it, take it to the creek, but don't let him go. I've got to get the hook out of its mouth." He watched as she positioned herself directly under him, and he cut the fishing line. With the squirming fish in one hand he held it over the net and asked, "Can you make strawberry short cake?"

"The best in the county. Dillon, please hurry before he dies. He can't live too much longer."

With careful aim he dropped the fish. A radiant smile lit up Elizabeth's face as she hurried to the stream. A fried-chicken dinner would be nice, Dillon realized, but seeing that beaming smile was worth any tree climb. Now if only he could get down without breaking any bones.

Elizabeth felt him walk up behind her as she softly petted the trapped fish. Turning her head she smiled and quickly placed a kiss on his cheek. "Thank you."

For the first time in eighteen years, thirty-six-year-old Dillon James McKenzie blushed.

Elizabeth closed her eyes trying to block out the pile of rafts, flippers, masks, boats, and two snorkel tubes; she counted to ten. When she opened her eyes, the pile hadn't disappeared. "Kevin and Kyle, I'm sorry, but all this stuff won't fit in my car."

Seeing the stubborn look on their faces she

tried changing her strategy. "How about if we take one thing today, and tomorrow we will bring something else?" The two red-headed boys, looking so much like their father, stared at the pile, back at the car, and finally back to Elizabeth. They were both dressed in bright Hawaiian-print bathing suits with wildly colored beach towels thrown over their shoulders. She smiled at Aaron, who was dressed in a solid-green suit and carrying an old bath towel that was frayed around the edges.

With a triumphant smile Kevin said, "I'll go get Dad's keys. We can take his van and fit all the stuff in it."

"Kevin, Kyle," came a roar from directly behind them. They had been so busy discussing the assortment of toys that no one had noticed Dillon coming around the side of the house.

Never in his entire life had he been so embarrassed. Here Elizabeth was helping him out by taking the boys to the pool, and they were arguing with her. "You two pick up every bit of your stuff and march your butts home."

"But, Dad!" they replied in unison.

"Now!" was roared so loud that Elizabeth thought it was probably heard in the next county. In what had taken the boys three trips to bring, they managed to carry back in one. Their faces registered shock as they struggled with their load.

Dillon saw the surprised look on her face and smiled weakly. "I've never denied them anything before. I'm sorry for the way they treated you. It won't happen again."

"It's okay, Dillon. They are only trying to see how far they can push."

"Well, they just hit the limit. Why don't you and Aaron go ahead without them today. I will talk to you later. Okay?"

She gave him an encouraging smile. "Okay. Don't

be too hard on them. I think your yelling did the trick."

Dillon had turned toward home when he noticed Aaron's face. His eyes, as dark as his mother's, stared at him in fear. He squatted down in front of Aaron. "Did my yelling scare you?"

With a hesitant step backward, Aaron nodded his head.

"You do know that I wasn't yelling at you, don't you, Aaron?"

"Yes, sir."

"You realize what Kevin and Kyle did was wrong. Your mother was taking them to the pool as a favor to me. What they did was rude; they both acted like the spoiled brats they're turning into." He smiled at Aaron. "If they both behave and apologize to your mother, maybe they can go with you tomorrow."

Uncertainty replaced the fear in Aaron's dark eyes. Dillon stood and stuck out his hand, "Let's shake on it, buddy." With a quick glance at his mother, Aaron stuck out his hand. "Hey, what's this?" With a look of surprise, Dillon asked, "What's that in your ear?" Flicking his wrist Dillon produced a shiny new quarter from behind Aaron's ear.

His dark shining eyes grew large with excitement. "Gee."

"Look, there's something behind the other ear too." Another flick of his wrist revealed a second quarter. Handing the coins to the beaming boy, Dillon smiled over at Elizabeth, who was busily watching her son rub behind his ears. "I don't see any more, but you can never tell when they might pop up again."

"Gee, thanks, Mr. McKenzie."

Dillon ruffled Aaron's hair. "You don't have to thank me. They came from your ears." Dillon remembered the last time he had done that trick on his boys; they had demanded to know why dollars didn't come out instead of quarters.

As Elizabeth watched Dillon calm Aaron, her heart lifted. He was obviously upset with his own sons' behavior, but he took the time to reassure Aaron. She flashed him a sincere smile of thanks as he stepped closer.

Whispering so Aaron couldn't overhear, he asked, "Do you want ice-cream money too?"

She smiled impishly. "Gee, Mr. McKenzie, that all depends on where you pull the quarters from."

Awareness flared in him, she was actually flirting. With a wicked grin he leaned closer and barely whispered, "What would you do if I could pull one out of . . ."

A pink tide ran up her cheeks, but she didn't break eye contact. "Get you a spot on Johnny Carson."

His husky laughter could still be heard after he placed a quick kiss on the end of her nose, waved good-bye to Aaron, and headed for home.

"Mom?" said Aaron.

As Elizabeth watched Dillon cut across her yard she absently answered her son. "Yes, Aaron?"

"Do you like Mr. McKenzie?"

With reluctance she turned her attention back to Aaron. Her voice softened as she asked, "Do you?"

"Gee, Mom. I think he's the greatest."

"So do I, Aaron. So do I," was whispered as she turned toward the car.

Drinking coffee in Elizabeth's kitchen could definitely become his favorite pastime. He watched as she bent over the oven and removed the third tray of cupcakes.

The boys and Rufus were running around in the adjoining yards, acting like a tribe of wild

Indians. The boys were trying to catch lightning bugs; Rufus was trying to eat them.

It wasn't until an hour after their usual supper time that Dillon had decided his boys had been punished enough. After a strong lecture on manners, he had left them in their rooms to think over everything he had said. Dinner had been so quiet he could, unfortunately, hear them chew their food.

For the first time in their young lives the boys loaded the dishwasher. Then Dillon explained what would come next. First they had to apologize to Mrs. Lancaster. If she accepted their apologies, they could go to the pool with her and Aaron . . . if they were invited.

From now on, Dillon decided, the boys would be assigned daily chores. At the end of the week, they would receive a small allowance. Everyone did his share of messing up the house; it wasn't fair that one person should clean it. They were a family, so from now on they all would have to pull their own weight.

After the kitchen was in order Dillon ushered his sons over to Elizabeth's for their formal apology. He wasn't surprised when she earnestly invited them swimming the next day and produced a freshly baked strawberry pie.

"Are you sure there's nothing I can help you with?" Dillon couldn't bring himself to go back home after the boys had deserted the kitchen in favor of the backyard. He settled in quite comfortably at her kitchen table and watched her work.

Elizabeth glanced up and smiled, "No. Thanks anyway." He had been sitting there for the past twenty minutes watching her intently. "What are you thinking?"

"How kissable you look."

With trembling hands she set the mixing bowl

on the counter. Sinking her teeth in her lower lip she continued to beat the thick batter in the bowl.

Dillon slowly stood up and walked toward her. She hadn't ordered him out of the house, which was a good sign. She also hadn't run toward him, thrown her arms around his neck, and declared undying love. But he could always hope.

She looked so darn cute dressed in yellow shorts and a yellow-and-white sleeveless blouse. Her hair was pulled back in its usual braid, and her skin held a touch of pink from too much sun at the pool. Coming up behind her, he gently removed the large bowl from her hands. Carefully turning Elizabeth by her shoulders, he trapped her between the counter and his body. He placed his hands on either side of her. Without touching her he said, "You are the most beautiful woman I've ever known, both inside and out."

"But—but you don't even know me." The words tumbled from her lips.

With a gentle finger he traced a path down her cheek to her lower lip. Softly running his finger over the small indentations caused by her teeth, he whispered, "Anyone can see you're beautiful on the outside, but it's the inside that's so important."

Elizabeth sucked in a breath as his finger ran over her lip. He'd called her beautiful. He might not have all his eggs in his basket, but he thought she was beautiful. Well, she'd never turned anyone to stone, and the last time she looked there weren't any snakes sprouting from her head, but "beautiful"? Nice, normal, ordinary, even plain would have been a better description. Heck, even her ex-husband never called her beautiful. With a start she realized that Dillon was still talking.

" . . . Slow because of the boys. They'd have to adjust to this."

"Slow? Boys? This?"

With a sexy smile, he said, "Us."

"Us?"

Chuckling, he said, "You're starting to sound like a parrot. Do you always repeat everything? I never noticed it before."

A feeling of uneasiness wavered in her stomach. What was he talking about? *Us?* There was no *us.* There was Aaron and her, and then there was Dillon, Kevin, and Kyle. But there definitely was no *us.*

Dillon read the emotions that crossed her face and sighed. Had he misread her response? How could she have kissed him like that yesterday and not felt the impact. Impact? Hell, it was more like running into a brick wall at sixty miles per hour.

He stepped back and gave Elizabeth some room. "I think I will drop the subject for now."

With every step he took backward, her mind started to clear. It was impossible to think logically with him so close. The best course of action would be to pretend this never happened and get back to her baking. "Excuse me, I have to get a pan from the pantry."

He watched the soft sway of her hips as she walked over to a closet door and went inside. With a curious fascination with everything she did, he followed. At one time the closet must have held a washer, dryer, and coatrack with enough room left over for storage. Now all three walls were lined with white shelves from floor to ceiling with a pull-string light in the middle.

He realized this must be the heart of Indescribably Delicious. There were bags of flour, sugar, and assorted baking ingredients. Pans of every conceivable size were lined up neatly in rows. When Elizabeth stretched up to reach for a pan on the top shelf, he said, "Allow me."

Expecting Dillon to reach for the pan, she was unprepared when his hands spanned her waist and he lifted her. With a startled gasp she blindly reached for the pan.

He carefully set her down and leaned against the doorjamb, effectively blocking her exit. He smiled, noticing the slight trembling of her hands, which were tightly grasping a rectangular pan. She wasn't as immune to his touch as she would have him believe. *Ah, Elizabeth,* he thought, *there will be an "us." Maybe not as fast as I would like, but soon.*

Elizabeth's eyes widened in alarm as Dillon blocked the door with his body. There was no way she could slip past, and stubborn pride kept her from asking. This was the one situation she should try to avoid . . . being alone with Dillon.

It wasn't that she distrusted him. Dillon was one of those rare men whom she knew instinctively she could trust. When she was in his arms, she felt safe. The world could crumble around her and she knew he would protect her. And there lay the danger.

She had been on her own for almost eight years and never relied on anyone. Her grandparents had lent support, understanding, and love, but not protection. After their deaths, she'd raised her son alone. Alone, she'd built Indescribably Delicious. And she wasn't sure she wanted her life to be any different.

What alarmed her about Dillon's blocking the exit to the pantry was her reaction to him. Every cell in her body knew when he was within ten feet of her and screamed for attention. Her hands trembled, aching to feel the texture of his hair again, and her lips quivered in anticipation of his kisses. A warm, womanly feeling settled in her stomach whenever she caught him looking at her in a certain way. These were very hazardous thoughts for a friend and neighbor.

Lifting her chin she stepped toward him. "Excuse me."

It defied the laws of physics that one little finger barely touching her lip could stop a 114-pound woman dead in her tracks.

He saw desire override caution in her dark eyes and silently vowed to go slow. With a prolonged movement he bent to taste her waiting lips . . . sweetness.

Feeling his gentle, coaxing lips moving over hers sent a wave of longing through her. Dillon felt the baking pan bounce off his sneaker and groaned as her arms slid around his waist. Her small dainty hands climbed his back to cling to wide shoulders as she deepened the kiss.

He willed himself again to slow down and think about his little toe, the one that might be broken. But when he felt the warmth of her tongue run over his lower lip, all thoughts of hospitals and casts evaporated. With a low groan he gently cupped her derriere and brought her in closer contact with his growing arousal.

With the strength of a desperate man, he broke the kiss and trailed a path down her throat with his lips till he ran into the barrier of her blouse. His voice was low and husky as he said, "This isn't working."

When she arched her back and subtly moved her hips he nearly went over the edge. "Elizabeth."

"Ummmm."

"I need your help here." He took a deep breath. "I'm a kiss away from making love to you. There are three very impressionable young boys in your backyard who could come in at any second. Not to mention Rufus, whose main objective in life is to eat your cat." Snapdragon had had several narrow escapes.

Slowly releasing her, he stepped back and ran a shaky hand through his hair. "I'm going to call my boys and head home because nothing I say right now will make sense. All I ask is that you please think about us?"

"Us?"

He gave her a quick kiss on the end of her nose. "Yeah, us." And he was gone.

Elizabeth stared out of the pantry into an empty kitchen, listening to Dillon talk to the boys out in the yard.

Us? There's no us. Now, why is that thought so depressing? she wondered.

Six

Brrrrring.

With an exasperated sigh Elizabeth wiped her hands on the dish towel and reached for the phone. "Indescribably delicious," she said.

"I know you are."

"Dillon?"

"Who else would know you're indescribably delicious?"

"I am?" After a moment's hesitation, she said, "No one. I mean, that's the name of my business."

"I know, Elizabeth." He chuckled.

"Oh."

"What are you and Aaron doing tonight?"

Now, why did a simple question like that cause her heart to beat faster? "Nothing, why?"

"Are you ready for your second lesson?" Dillon asked in a low, intimate voice.

Elizabeth closed her eyes and pictured Dillon giving her a lesson on the soft quilt that covered her bed. Moonlight was streaming in through the window as Dillon was braced above her. "Yes," she said.

"Good. We'll pick you and Aaron up around four.

Wear long pants—it gets cool at night—and bring jackets. Dinner will be on me tonight."

"Where are we going?"

"It's a surprise. Believe me, it's a must for a fatherhood lesson."

At six-thirty that evening Elizabeth found herself sitting near first base at Veteran's Stadium. In one hand she clutched a hotdog with the works, and in the other a huge coke. The boys were bouncing up and down on their seats with excitement. They'd already finished their hotdogs, cokes, pretzels, and one of everything else the vendors were selling.

Aaron stared at his surroundings sipping a cola. He was wearing his free give-away Phillies watch. After a motherly smile to the boys, Elizabeth turned to the man sitting beside her.

Tonight he was dressed in worn jeans and a green plaid shirt, his jeans jacket having been thrown over the back of his seat. He turned to her and smiled. "Aaron seems to be enjoying himself. How about you?"

She swallowed the last mouthful of her hotdog. "Very much, but the game hasn't started yet."

"It will in a couple of minutes. Have you ever been here before?"

"No. My grandfather used to watch all the Phillies' games on the television, so I understand the sport. I've just never been to a game before."

With a tender smile he pushed a stray hair behind her ear. "Let me know if you don't understand something; I'll try to explain it the best I can. I hope all the yelling and screaming won't bother you. It tends to get very vocal in the stands, especially if the game is a close one."

"I'm sure I won't mind. But I do have one little question."

"What's that?"

"Who are we playing?"

Dillon laughed so hard he barely got the answer out. "The Saint Louis Cardinals."

An hour later Dillon couldn't have pried the smile off his face with a crowbar. The game had started on time, and after the first inning the score was zip to zip. By the second inning the score was tied one all. The third inning proved very interesting: Elizabeth not only knew the sport, she had some definite opinions about how it should be played.

At the top of the fourth, she single-handedly cheered on the pitcher. The score was still tied at one apiece, but the bats were starting to crack. The Phillies had two outs, a runner on second and third. A line drive was hit to the short stop, who threw it to first. The call was close; it could have gone either way. The umpire jerked his thumb over his shoulder. The runner was out.

Elizabeth jumped up, spilling half of her popcorn, and screamed he was safe. A bald-headed man three rows down stood up and shouted to Elizabeth, "You tell him, lady." By the top of the eighth the score was Phillies 3, Cardinals 2, and if Elizabeth had anything to do with it, Dillon figured it would stay that way.

Dillon watched as Aaron stared at his mother as if he had never seen her before. Obviously she'd never screamed at anyone before in her life. Who was this gorgeous firebrand who had half their section agreeing with every call she made? With silent amusement Dillon sat low in his chair and watched the play of emotions across her face. Joy brightened her eyes, and when she concentrated she always sank her teeth into her lower lip. Anger caused a flush to tint her cheeks, and total astonishment at some of the calls caused her mouth to hang open.

Shifting in his seat, Dillon wondered what it

would feel like to have all the passion she directed toward the game centered on him.

After another crack of a bat he watched as St. Louis tied the score. The ball was thrown to second to pick off the runner coming from first. The head-first slide kicked up dust and Elizabeth's temper.

Elizabeth watched the umpire spread his arms in the safe sign, then yelled toward the field, "Are you blind? He was out."

Dillon's silent chuckle died in his throat as a beer-bellied man wearing a Cardinal's T-shirt stood up and shouted, "Shut up, lady, and sit down."

If Elizabeth had thought about it, she probably would have quietly sat. But excitement was pouring through her veins, and she was having the time of her life. So she shouted back, "Any idiot could see he was out."

Dillon groaned when the Cardinals' fan put down his huge cup of beer. He was going to jail; he could see it all now. The guy would come over, and he would have to deck the jerk. Here he was giving her fatherhood lessons, and he was already blowing it.

As Dillon slowly rose to his feet to confront the irate fan, at least twelve other defenders rose behind him. It looked like Dillon's sweet, sexy neighbor wasn't going to start a fistfight; she was going to initiate a brawl.

But when Dillon stood to his full six-feet-one height next to Elizabeth, the irate fan apparently reconsidered. "Forget it. It's not worth it," he mumbled, as he slowly sat down.

Elizabeth slowly sat back in her seat as a tide of humiliation swept up her cheeks. She didn't notice Dillon sitting back down. She hadn't even noticed him stand. She was too mortified. She'd actually called some guy an idiot. Oh, Lord, she had never said anything like that before, not even to her ex-husband, who had deserved it.

Dillon noticed her embarrassment and figured the new Elizabeth was gone for now. But he knew she'd be back; he had plans for her once they left the stadium. "Aaron doesn't play baseball does he?" Dillon asked.

With downcast eyes she mumbled, "No."

A cold shudder shot through him as he thought of her cheering in some bleachers as her son played on the field. If she was this riled up over a bunch of men she'd never met, he couldn't begin to imagine what she'd do if Aaron was called out. "Thank God," he said.

It was after two in the morning when Dillon noticed that her lights were still on . . . again. He didn't think anything was wrong. But it did seem strange. It had been after eleven when they arrived home from the game, which the Phillies had won. All three boys had fallen asleep in the back seat, and Elizabeth was quiet, fighting the sandman all the way home. So why were her lights still on three hours later?

He made a quick trip upstairs to make sure the boys were sleeping soundly. He patted Rufus, who was sleeping at the foot of Kevin's bed. "Protect the house, Rufus." Rufus rolled over on his back, spread all four limbs and began to snore. With a quick scratch and a chuckle, Dillon left his boys in good hands and headed over to Elizabeth's.

With a jerk Elizabeth's chin slid out of the palm of her hand and her eyes flew open. What had woken her? She knew sleeping at the kitchen table wasn't exactly beauty rest, but darn she was tired. The last cake was in the oven, and when the buzzer sounded she was heading for cool cotton sheets and dreamland. But the buzzer hadn't sounded, so what had disturbed her?

The knock on the back door caused her to blink sleep out of her eyes. A hurried glance at the clock on the stove told her that it was almost two-thirty; the cake had twenty minutes left to bake and someone was knocking at her door. She tried to decide what to do. No one had ever knocked on her door past ten at night, let alone two-thirty in the morning.

The knock sounded again, this time a bit louder and more demanding. With nervous fingers she grabbed her biggest butcher knife and slowly walked toward the door. Where were her brains? Wasn't she the same person who had always yelled, during a late-night movie, at some stupid coed for going to the basement when she heard strange noises? A quick glance toward the living room showed everything to be in order. What in the world was she supposed to do now? She couldn't sneak out of the house; Aaron was sleeping in his bed.

Taking a deep breath, she stood against the back door with its yellow ruffled curtains and raised the knife. "Who's there?"

"Elizabeth, it's me, Dillon. Open the door."

Trembling with relief she threw open the door and rushed toward him.

She was a step away when Dillon noticed the lethal butcher knife clutched in her raised hand. Instinctively he stopped, dropped, and rolled . . . right down the two wooden steps that led to her door.

A silent scream rose in her throat as she watched helplessly as Dillon tumbled down the steps. Her eyes widened in horror as he lay motionless, his feet on the slate path to her door, his head and upper body in the soft grass, and his left arm laid

across three petunias that had given their lives to
soften the blow.

With disgust she looked at the knife still clutched
in her trembling hand. With a shiver of revulsion
she dropped the butcher knife and watched it fall
harmlessly to the wooden deck.

Oh, Lord, she'd hurt him. Her feet flew down
the steps as she ran toward Dillon. Cautiously
she cradled his head in her lap and whispered his
name. "Dillon?"

Dillon dimly heard his name and felt gentle fingers touch his face. This was definitely heaven,
and he wasn't moving.

"Please, Dillon, answer me."

Why was Elizabeth upset? He slowly opened his
eyes.

In the pale light streaming from the open kitchen
door he watched her dark eyes pool with tears.
She was dressed in a white cotton gown with lace
trim, and her dark hair was cascading over her
shoulders as she bent her head over him. In that
moment Dillon knew he had found heaven. He
loved her. He hadn't been looking for love; he just
happened to move next door to it.

He reached up and gently cradled the back of
her head. Slowly he brought her lips down to his.
He captured her mouth before she could speak.

Heat spiraled through her as he deepened the
kiss. When his tongue ran over her lower lip she
moaned. In one smooth movement she found herself lying on the dew-covered grass with Dillon
above her. A groan escaped her lips as Dillon
broke the kiss and lovingly brushed back the hair
clinging to her face. Desire burned in his green
eyes. "Touch me, Elizabeth. Feel what you do to
me."

With trembling fingers she reached up and caressed his unshaven jaw. Lightly running her fingers across his parted lips, she heard his sudden

intake of breath and smiled. He was feeling the same fever that gripped her. With prolonged slowness she trailed her fingers down his chin, over the strong column of his throat, and came to a halt when a button barred her way.

Feeling her fingers faintly caress his skin nearly broke his control. He rested his weight on his forearms and took a deep breath. With a husky voice he said, "Unbutton it."

Her fingers fumbled their way through all six buttons before she allowed herself to touch his chest. She placed both palms on the dark hair that partially covered his chest. Feeling the downy softness of the hair, she ran her fingers through it with awe. He had the most incredible chest— firm and muscular but covered with soft skin. She explored it till she encountered the cold metal of his belt buckle. Startled by the sudden chill, she stopped and her eyes flew up to his.

Dillon had watched the emotions play across her face; desire, awe, curiosity, and finally uncertainty. He wanted to tell her to unbutton that too. He'd died if she didn't. Then again he would probably have heart failure if she did.

He wrapped a strand of her hair around his finger. In the faint light he could see the rapid rise and fall of her breast. Soft womanly mounds lay under the deceptive innocence of white cotton. The gown she wore was designed for a lady, but the shadows of hardened nipples were definitely those of a woman.

Releasing the lock of hair, he gently traced her lower lip, then caressed her jaw and neck till he reached the barrier of a row of small white buttons that ran down the front of her gown. He slowly worked the five tiny buttons through their holes before parting the gown and gazing at the treasure he uncovered. "Beautiful doesn't begin to describe you, Elizabeth."

She could feel the thundering of his heart beneath her hand. It matched the tempo of her own. The cool night breeze floated across her feverish breasts as he gently cupped them and brought his mouth down. With a flick of his tongue he brought a hardening peak to its fully glory. As he paid tribute to the other nipple she clutched the warm shoulders beneath his shirt and arched her back. A moan vibrated in his throat as he gently tugged at her breast. Need spread like fire within her as his mouth blazed a trail down her stomach. In the far recesses of her mind a persistent hum surfaced above her hazy thoughts.

He raised his head when he felt her stiffen in his arms. "Elizabeth?"

Her voice was tense. "I hear something."

A sexy grin spread across Dillon's face. "Rockets? Fireworks?"

"Alarm clocks."

He chuckled devilishly. "I think I'd better try harder." He was lowering his head to recapture a moist peak when he heard the buzzing sound. He turned his head toward the open kitchen door. "It's coming from your kitchen."

"Oh, good Lord, my cake."

He was unprepared for the gentle push she gave him, and in surprise he allowed her to slide out from under him and run toward the kitchen. He turned over on his back, staring up at the stars. Why did she have to be baking a cake while he was making love to her?

Finding no answer in the sky, he turned his head and stared at his house. Everything looked so peaceful and quiet from the outside; he wished it had been true of Elizabeth's kitchen. He gingerly rose to his feet. Now that Elizabeth had left, every muscle protested, aching from the fall.

She had just taken the third cake pan from the oven when Dillon entered the kitchen and closed the door behind him. The cake was perfect, but she wasn't so sure about their friendship. "Are you hurt?"

He smiled ruefully. The lady was back in charge. "Nothing a cold shower couldn't cure." She turned to concentrate on the cake pans. "I'm sorry, Elizabeth. That was crude. I'm fine." She looked at him skeptically. "Really."

"Then would you mind explaining what happened?" she asked.

Dillon looked at the flush in her cheeks, the kiss-swollen lips, and the tangled mane of dark hair. His eyes lingered on the dark shadows of her kiss-moistened nipples that the white gown clung to. In her eyes he saw stubborn pride as well as vulnerability. "Before or after you charged me with a meat cleaver?"

"I did not." Seeing him arch a cinnamon-colored brow in disbelief, she said, "Well, I did have a small knife in my hand, and I guess I kind of ran out the door."

"Why?"

"Because you scared the living tar out of me. No one ever knocks on anyone's door at two-thirty in the morning around here. I didn't know who in tarnation it was." In a softer voice she said, "I didn't know what else to do."

Dillon crossed the room in four strides and gathered her in his arms. He heard the fright in her voice and regretted causing it. "I'm sorry for scaring you, honey. You were right to be scared, though. Never open your door to someone that late at night. Next time call the police or better yet keep my number by the phone and call me."

Feeling protected and safe in his arms restored her sense of humor. "How could I call you if you're the one knocking?"

"Point taken. How about if we make up a code?" Feeling her nod against his chest he continued,

"Just for the record, that little bitsy knife you were wielding like a samurai warrior could be used to behead terrorists."

"That still doesn't explain your suicide roll down my steps."

"Well, umm . . ."

Hearing the hesitation in his voice she pulled out of his arms. "Did you really think I was going to use the knife on you?"

"If I had had time to think about it, I know you wouldn't. It just happened so fast. And let me tell you that knife picked up a pretty strange gleam from the moon. I acted on instinct—stop, drop, and roll."

She laughed. "Dillon, you use stop, drop, and roll when you're on fire, not when someone attacks you with a knife."

With sudden seriousness he gently cupped her chin. "Then you better get used to seeing me doing it, because every time I kiss you I catch fire." He ran a hand through his hair, trying to maintain his self-control. "Like I told you before, we'll take it slow and easy. If it were just me and you I would take off the kid gloves, but we have to think about the boys, yours and mine. I want you more than any other woman I've ever known. I'm usually a very patient man, but I'm not sure how long I can last against you." He caressed her cheek lightly. "I'll try to wait until you're sure."

He placed one last kiss on her slightly parted lips. "Good night, Elizabeth, sweet dreams."

Her mumbled good-night followed him across the kitchen. His hand was on the doorknob when her voice stopped him. "Dillon? Are you sure?"

"One-hundred-and-ten percent." Then he was gone.

• • •

At nine o'clock the next morning Elizabeth was trying to concentrate on the cake she was icing, not Dillon. She had one last cake to decorate, then she would make her deliveries and do her shopping. With any luck, she hoped it would pour rain, as the weatherman had predicted. If it did, then she could catch a short nap before making the chicken dinner she'd promised Dillion in exchange for saving her fish. Stifling a yawn she muttered, "So who cares if I didn't get any sleep last night? Life goes on."

She blindly reached for her cup of coffee while staring at the sickest-looking flowers she'd ever drawn on icing. They reminded her of the trampled pansies of just a few short days ago. With a grimace she picked up a butter knife and scraped the mutant roses off the cake. She'd do them over and try to keep her mind on the task at hand this time.

By lunchtime the deliveries and shopping were done, and it was raining. She sent Aaron over to Dillon's to tell him dinner would be at six. Just as she finished putting away the groceries the phone rang. "Indescribably Delicious," she answered.

"Do you always talk dirty on the phone?"

"Only to suicidal maniacs who scare defenseless ladies at two in the morning."

A hearty chuckle came over the line. "Defenseless?"

"Around you I am."

Dillon heard the serious tone of her voice and gripped the phone harder. "It works both ways, Elizabeth."

She wanted to laugh but didn't. What in the world would Dillon have to be on guard about? She was the one who was going to end up with a broken heart if she wasn't careful. He wanted to go to bed with her, plain and simple.

But plain and simple weren't in her vocabulary

when she thought of Dillon. Love, need, and forever were her priorities. After climbing into her lonely bed the night before, she'd admitted to herself she loved him. She just didn't know what to do about it. She wanted to ignore it, but could she ignore love? It would be like trying to ignore a tsunami wave.

If she followed her heart and made love with Dillon, could she live if he rejected her afterward? Her only lover had been her husband, and he had rejected her in every way. It did not inspire confidence.

"Elizabeth?"

"I'm sorry. I must have been daydreaming."

"That's okay." He knew when to change the subject. "The reason I'm calling is to ask if Aaron can go with me and the boys. I promised to paint their rooms this week, and they get to pick out the colors."

"Sure, as long as Aaron wants to go."

"He said if it's okay with you. We'll also be stopping at a couple of other stores. I'm buying carpeting for the boys' rooms before they ruin the wooden floors. I caught them wearing roller skates this morning. They were playing hockey in Kevin's room."

"Oh, my!"

"Rufus was refereeing, and guess what they were using for a puck?"

"Please tell me it wasn't Boris," she said, referring to the boys' hamster.

"No, they weren't using anything live, at least it isn't any longer." He laughed.

"Yuk, I don't think I want to hear any more of this."

"It's not that bad. Well, it was at one time. Last year their Uncle Shane noticed the boys' preoccupation with war, guts, and blood, that sort of thing. For Kevin's birthday he bought him unarmed hand grenades. I didn't think anything about them at the time. You could go to the toy store and buy plastic replicas. Anyway, back then I employed an older woman, Mrs. Snodgrass, to take care of the boys and the condo while I went to work. I came home one evening to find her hiding behind the couch with a cooking pot on her head babbling something about Rambo and first blood. Needless to say she gave me her notice, effective immediately. The grenades were put away, and both terrorists were severely reprimanded, along with their uncle." With laughter in his voice, he said, "I haven't seen them since until today when one rolled down the stairs. Gave me quite a scare until Kyle yelled, 'Goal scored for the Commando team.' "

Elizabeth started to laugh. "What you are so nicely telling me is that if a grenade comes sailing into my kitchen, not to panic."

"I'm trying to warn you about Kevin and Kyle, but you're on your own when I'm not around."

"Gee, thanks a lot. Did Aaron tell you dinner is at six?"

"Yes, but you don't really have to cook dinner just because I saved your fish."

Elizabeth smiled. He was giving her a chance to back out. "A promise is a promise. See you and the boys at six. Tell Aaron to behave himself, okay?"

"Aaron always behaves himself. See you tonight."

She hung up the phone and smiled. The entire afternoon was hers. With a yawn she headed for the bedroom and a nap. Curling up on the old-fashioned, yellow patchwork quilt, she heard the sound of falling rain and shouts from the boys as Dillon ushered them into his van. It was sweet of him to take Aaron along, though it would have been sweeter if he had invited her. She just might give up a couple of hours sleep to be in his company. Who was she kidding? She'd give up another night's sleep and then some for his company. He was nice and friendly on the phone; that meant he wasn't too upset about last night, didn't it? Why should be he upset? She was distressed enough for them both.

With a determined punch to her pillow she forced Dillon from her mind and concentrated on counting sheep. She couldn't cook a decent meal if she couldn't keep her eyes open.

Seven

Elizabeth stared at the microwave with a disgusted frown. So this was the wave of the future. She didn't like it. There was something sinister about the black box, although she couldn't pinpoint what it was just yet. But it was there; she could feel it. She looked through the glass door and watched the paper bag full of popcorn jerk every second or so. She knew that this popcorn could not possibly be as good as hers. She and Aaron had spent many nights in the dead of winter sitting in front of their fireplace, munching on popcorn. Sometimes they cooked hotdogs on long sticks and had picnics on the living room rug.

Despite her attitude toward the microwave, she liked Dillon's kitchen. She had to admit he really had put a lot of work into the house this past month. His office was now tastefully done in shades of green that gave the room a peaceful, homey feeling. Kevin's room was painted beige and had a brown carpet to protect the oak floor. On the walls were posters of various stars, from skateboarding to the latest blockbuster movie. His curtains and comforter supported the local football team, and a bookcase that touched the ceiling helped hold an array of toys.

Kyle's room had a prehistoric theme: dinosaurs, which covered the curtains, bedspread, and walls. A dark green rug prevented any more roller derby games, and a bookcase matching Kevin's held assorted toys, primarily dinosaurs. The only other room on the second floor she'd been in was a large bathroom. It was still papered in faded pink roses with an antique tub and sink. The toilet was a repulsive shade of pink that spoke of a lack of funds or taste or both.

She glanced around the kitchen and smiled with satisfaction. She had helped to decorate it. Two weeks ago Dillon had shown up on her back stoop with tickets to a stock car race. He called it an important fatherhood lesson and explained he wasn't sure when he'd be able to find time for the next lesson because he had to get back to work; vacation was over.

In the middle of crowded bleachers, eating the greasiest hamburger and fries she'd ever tasted, he'd explained that he really wanted to have the kitchen redecorated before resuming his work, but frankly the color scheme had him puzzled. Elizabeth had wanted to spend as much time with him as possible. So, as the cars screamed around the track and the smell of burning rubber filled her nostrils, she had agreed to help decorate his kitchen.

The following Saturday, after her deliveries, she and Aaron had found themselves in the nearest mall searching for curtains, tablecloths, placemats, and anything else that belonged in a country kitchen. With a list of measurements and a color sample of the yellow paint she'd chosen, she had attacked each store with military precision.

Cobalt-blue plaid curtains with a matching tablecloth had been dumped in Dillon's arms. Placemats in the same fabric had been declared perfect for his pine table and handed to Kyle. Aaron had carried a wrought-iron contraption that she explained to Dillon would be hung from the ceiling for his cooper pots. Two throw rugs had been placed in Kevin's arms, and she had pulled up the rear carrying a centerpiece of silk daisies.

She liked the finished effect. The room was relaxing, the type of kitchen someone wouldn't mind drinking a second cup of coffee in.

The loud beep of the microwave brought her attention back to the popcorn and the party at hand. Tonight would be the first time Aaron had ever slept away from home. After she had helped carry over a sleeping bag, a pillow, and a stuffed tote bag, her motherly concern made her stall. Half an hour later she had been confined to the kitchen and ordered by three vocal boys to bring on the snacks.

Dillon had handed her a box of popcorn and, after a quick kiss on the end of her nose, went to set up the tape he'd rented for the VCR. With a sigh she reached into the oven and pulled out the steaming hot bag and dumped the contents into a large bowl. Ever since the night Dillon had fallen down the steps and almost made love to her in the back yard, he hadn't kissed her. Occasionally he'd brushed his lips across her cheek, or had given her a hurried peck, but he'd never again given her a real kiss. And she wanted a full-bodied, curl-your-toes kiss.

She needed to feel his arms surround her, his heat engulf her. She burned with the desire to feel him fill the void deep within her.

She loved him. She loved his gentleness and understanding. She admired his sense of humor and his ability to laugh at himself. His kisses drove her wild, and the feel of his hands caressing her ignited a fire only he could extinguish. So why had he stopped kissing her? Was he bored with her already, or wasn't he sure he wanted her anymore?

Dillon walked into the kitchen, hoping to help her with the snacks. He noticed the flush on her cheeks and stopped when desire-filled eyes stared back at him. Oh, Lord, what was she thinking? His fingers clenched into a fist, and he swallowed the lump in his throat. "Are you almost done? The movie's ready to start."

Elizabeth watched his face harden, and sighed. This was the unknown Dillon, the unapproachable one. He looked as if she were made of stone. She couldn't read any expression on his face. "Yes, all I need are the drinks." She took a deep breath. "Maybe I should go home and leave you guys alone."

"Don't be silly. The boys were looking forward to your staying a little while."

She wasn't sure what he meant. The boys wanted her to stay, but what about him? "Okay, I'll stay for a while."

Taking a deep breath, Dillon forced his hands to relax. Seeing such desire in her eyes caused a very basic male response. For the past month he had fought against the fire that raced through him every time he came close to her. She needed time, and by hell he was going to give it to her, even if he went crazy doing it. He smiled a friendly smile. "Why don't you carry in the popcorn. I'll get the drinks."

"Okay. What movie did you rent?"

"*Pee Wee's Great Adventure* and *Grizzly.*"

"*Grizzly?*"

There was a mischievous gleam in his eyes. "It's a story about a grizzly bear who starts eating campers."

"You're not going to show that to the boys are you?"

"Nope, it's for me."

She shuddered in disgust. "Sick, Dillon, real sick."

They spent the next two hours cheering Pee Wee on in his search for his bike. The boys lay on the floor devouring sodas, popcorn, and an entire bowl of chips. She and Dillon ended up on the couch very close to each other but not touching.

She clutched her drink, watching the ice cubes in her ginger ale melt. Shifting nervously she tried to concentrate on the movie and forget about where she was sitting. When what seemed like the longest movie in her life finally ended, the boys headed upstairs, taking Dillon with them.

Elizabeth was picking up the empty popcorn bowl and soda cans when Dillon came back downstairs. "All tucked in?" she asked.

"Put that stuff down, Elizabeth. You could have come up with me to say good night."

"No. It's Aaron's first time away and I think he wants to be treated like a big boy."

He walked over to her and took the soda cans. "Why don't I go put on a pot of coffee?"

She nervously glanced down at her sneakers. "I should be going home."

"Why don't you stay a while?" When she hesitated he played his ace in the hole. "Aaron might need you."

She listened to the soft giggles coming from the second floor. The boys sounded perfectly happy; there was no real reason for her to stay. Was Dillon just being neighborly or was he trying to keep her there? When she looked back at him she noticed that his smile seemed friendly. But there was a hint of something else lurking in the depths of his eyes. "Okay, I will stay for a while. Do you need any help with the coffee?"

"No, but you can keep me company."

He made the coffee and unearthed a bag of fig bars. He started the tape and sat down in the middle of the couch, placing his arm behind her. Noticing her raised eyebrow, he said, "That's in case you get scared, you can throw yourself at me."

"Only if I get scared?" she said, amused.

The laughter left his eyes. She was beautiful, with her long dark hair and her sun-kissed skin. Her large brown eyes sparkled with life, and a smile tilted up the corners of her sensual mouth. A large red shirt covered her from collar to midthigh. The sleeves were rolled back to below her elbows, and a wide silver belt clinched it at the waist. A pair of faded jeans hugged her every curve, and gleaming white sneakers completed the outfit.

He loved her. He loved her smile and gentleness. Her air of innocence nearly drove him insane. He was determined to be the man to breech that barrier. She was proud, stubborn, and fair minded. She had raised a son anyone would be proud to call his own. She had single-handedly started a business that supported her and Aaron. Elizabeth Lancaster was every man's fantasy rolled up in one petite package, and he wanted her.

Heat coiled low in his stomach as he thought of her throwing herself in his arms. For the past month he'd kept things light and friendly to give her time, but things seemed to have changed. He tenderly pulled on her braid. "Naw, I'm easy. You can throw yourself in my arms anytime."

She was working up the courage to take him up on his offer, when the sounds of laughter and barking reached her ears. The boys were still up and probably would be for quite a while yet. She cautiously reached for her cup and watched the movie. Two beautiful girls pitched their tent high in the mountains. It didn't look good. "Is there going to be a lot of blood?" she asked.

"I've never seen this one before. Pay attention

though. It's training for your final exam in father-hood."

"Grizzlies?"

"No, camping. Your final test will be a camping trip in the great outdoors."

She was horrified. "With grizzlies?"

"Not unless you want to go to Canada." He laughed. "Grizzly bears are pretty scarce in the States and nonexistent on the east coast, except in zoos."

She turned her attention back to the screen where the girls were now building a blazing fire. As the girls cooked hotdogs and talked about their latest boyfriends, a few small rabbits scampered through the underbrush. Smiling, Elizabeth thought she could handle camping. "When are we going?"

Dillon heard the excitement in her voice. "I was thinking fall, when it's cooler." He also thought of cold nights snuggling deep in a sleeping bag with her. By fall their relationship should be estab-lished; he'd be a raving lunatic by then if she still wasn't sure.

The setting sun disappeared behind the tree-covered mountain turning the sky a brilliant red. The girls rolled out sleeping bags and kicked dirt over the fire. Elizabeth was taking a demure sip of coffee when a huge paw practically took the blond coed's face off.

Dillon wasn't sure who screamed louder, the defaced blonde or Elizabeth. Hot coffee and cup went flying as she flew in his arms and buried her head. The roar of the grizzly camouflaged his laugh-ter as he held the trembling woman in his arms. He reached for the remote control and turned off the sound as the petite brunette went screaming into the woods with the grizzly in fast pursuit.

"Elizabeth, it's only a movie."

"Oh, sweet Mary, did you see the blood?"

She felt a suspicious shaking of his shoulders.

"No, honey, I didn't see any blood. I saw ketchup, a rubber mask, and a fake bear paw."

"Sick, Dillon, real sick." She raised her face and looked into his smiling face. "How can you watch movies like that?"

"It was the only one they had about camping."

"And you expected me to go camping after seeing that?"

He gently pulled her the rest of the way onto his lap and pushed back a stray wisp of dark hair. "Sure, you know it's fake. Camping will be fun. Where do you want to go?"

She looked at him seriously. "Disneyland. I want Bambi, Flower, and Thumper in my woods."

He looked at her pout and burst out laughing. With a quick series of light kisses he tried to erase the sulk. Then he drew back to examine his effectiveness. The pout was still present, but her gaze belied unhappiness.

Elizabeth watched the amusement fade from Dillon's eyes. With a trembling hand she threaded her fingers through his hair and brought his lips back to hers. When he didn't respond, she pulled back and opened her eyes.

She saw raw need burning in the depths of his gaze. "Elizabeth, are you sure?"

She smiled shyly. "One-hundred-and-ten per-cent."

With gentle hands Dillon picked her up and carefully placed her on the sofa next to him. In a harsh whisper he explained, "The boys are still awake. Until they fall asleep you are to sit over there and not make a sound. Don't touch me, don't talk to me, and for pete's sake don't look at me. We are going to watch television." After delivering his message he pressed a series of buttons on the remote control and sat back down. A news program filled the television screen.

Elizabeth watched the colors blur on the screen

as tears filled her eyes. What had gone wrong? Wasn't *he* sure? Talk about embarrassing moments, you throw yourself at the man you love and he prefers Walter Cronkite, or whoever that was spouting gloom and doom. Rapidly blinking her eyes to clear her vision, she stared as the entire newsroom wished everyone a good-night, and then a commercial for roach traps blared into the room.

Great, her whole life just unraveled and she was supposed to set up little hotels for bugs.

Elizabeth bit her lip to stop a sigh from escaping. The digital clock on the VCR revealed that twenty minutes had crept by since Dillon told her not to move. Not a sound had come from the boys upstairs, which meant they were either sleeping or had tied sheets together and escaped. What was she supposed to do, sit here all night?

She straightened her back, lifted her chin, and watched as Mr. Ed talked to Wilbur. Pride was such a terrible thing. To be humiliated and forced to watch Mr. Ed find an orthodontist at the same time was too much to bear. With trembling legs she rose from the couch and walked toward the door, without saying a word.

Dillon had just finished mentally listing all the ways he was going to love Elizabeth. He'd start by unbraiding her long dark hair, spreading it out across his pillow, and he wouldn't stop until he'd tasted every inch of her luscious body. The movement next to him brought his eyes open. Elizabeth was leaving!

Her hand was on the doorknob pulling the door open when his palm stopped its movement. "Where are you going?"

Elizabeth heard the surprise in his voice and wondered what he expected her to do. Not taking her eyes off the door she muttered, "Home."

Astonishment raised his voice. "Why?"

Her hand turned white with anger as she gripped the knob. "Because I hate *Mr. Ed* reruns." What in the world was he doing?

"*Mr. Ed?*"

She might be trying to hold onto pride, but patience just went flying. Glaring up at him, she explained in the tone of voice a parent used with children, "The stupid show you are watching."

A tide of red swept up his cheeks. "I wasn't watching television."

Intrigued by his blush, she hesitated. "What were you doing?"

Holding her eyes he answered honestly, "Thinking of all the ways I'm going to love you, as soon as the boys fall asleep."

"Oh."

"Yeah, oh." He watched desire flair in those dark pools. "First is your hair." With great care he unfastened the rubberband and slowly ran his fingers through the long tresses cascading down her back. "Beautiful, just like I remembered it."

"Oh."

A hungry look appeared in her eyes as he traced her lower lip with the pad of his thumb. "In my dreams your hair is spread out over my pillow."

"Oh."

A smile broke across his face. "Talkative tonight, are you?" He bent down and placed a quick kiss on her moist lips. "Am I going to get my dream tonight, Elizabeth?"

She watched emotions burn in his eyes: desire, hunger, need, and something else. Could it be love? With a smile she closed the front door and turned the lock. "We both get our dreams tonight."

Heat twisted low in his abdomen. "If I kiss you now, we'll never make it upstairs." Grabbing her hand he led her through the kitchen, switching off the coffeepot and light on their way. The television and the last remaining lights downstairs were extinguished before Dillon picked her up and carried her upstairs.

Nestled in the safety of his arms Elizabeth smiled; heaven was indeed upward. At the top of the stairs he started toward Kevin's room. Her eyebrow raised as he slowly set her back on her feet in front of Kevin's door. A curious glance inside confirmed all three boys were in their sleeping bags sound asleep. Rufus, in his usual guard position, was sound asleep on Kevin's bed.

Dillon watched as she looked into the room, a motherly smile lighting up her face. It was directed not just at Aaron but to his sons as well. The first major obstacle had been hurdled in his quest to make her his. She'd accepted his sons; the boys generally liked each other, and he could love Aaron as his own if she let him. Lovingly he raised her hand to his lips and placed a soft kiss in her palm before cupping his jaw with it.

In a heartbeat her smile turned from motherly to womanly. No words were spoken as she lowered her hand and tenderly placed it in his. Side by side they walked down the hall toward the master suite.

The soft click of the lock sounded loud in the dark room. Elizabeth stood absolutely still as Dillon moved off to find a light. She quickly glanced around his room for the first time. The nightstand was piled high with magazines, a pair of brown-framed glasses perched on top. She realized Dillon must wear glasses while reading.

He obviously hadn't redone this room since moving in. Faded wallpaper boasted roses in a sickly shade of peach, and lace curtains worn and torn with time hung at the windows. A sitting room opened up directly onto the master bedroom. In the darkness she could barely make out a pair of French doors that led to a balcony, which she knew overlooked the back yard. There was no furniture in the sitting room.

The king-size bed drew her attention; it looked like an antique with its four posts reaching well over six feet high. A delicate wood-framed canopy arched another foot over the posts. A hand-crocheted coverlet, as fine as a spider's wed, draped the canopy. It was enchanting, whimsical, and romantic. The only other furniture in the room was a pine armoire.

Dillon noticed her preoccupation with his bed and smiled. "You like it? I bought it the week after I purchased the house. They seemed to go together."

"It's lovely. You *are* a romantic."

He stepped over to her and gently cupped the back of her head. He ran his fingers deep into her hair as he brought his lips a breath away from hers and whispered, "From now on I'm going to show you just how romantic I can be." Then he brought his mouth down to hers.

Hunger spiraled through her as her arms encircled his neck. The faintest pressure on his tongue opened her mouth to the sweet pleasure of his kiss. A moan of despair escaped her lips as he broke contact with them and trailed a path of kisses to her ear. With trembling fingers she removed the dangling silver and turquoise earrings, dropping them to the floor.

The sound caused Dillon to raise his lips from her throat. A faint smile pulled at her mouth as she reached for the front of his gray shirt. One by one buttons were released revealing his chest. With hands that shook she pushed the shirt off his shoulders and down his muscular arms. She ran fingers through irresistible downy hair that feathered his chest, and closed her eyes.

Elizabeth's hands on his chest brought Dillon out of his daze. She had taken off his shirt. Reining in the wild feelings she was causing, he slowly undid her silver and turquoise belt and dropped it on top of his shirt.

How could she possibly be this beautiful? In the low light, wearing an oversized red shirt with her hair a tangled array that hung to her waist, she was gorgeous. Large brown eyes were bright with passion, and moist lips begged for kisses. She'd never looked move lovely than at this moment. "You're beautiful." Watching the blush sweep up her cheeks he said with hardened desire, "And you're mine."

Elizabeth observed his expression as he slowly undid the buttons on her blouse. As each button was freed, want, need, and desire were clearly visible in his eyes. With great care he slowly pushed the blouse off her shoulders. Hunger burned bright in his green eyes as he reached for the front clasp of her transparent white lace bra. Was he really seeing her—plain, ordinary Elizabeth?

Suddenly she didn't feel plain or ordinary anymore. How could she when Dillon looked at her like that? She reached for his gleaming belt buckle with renewed confidence and slowly unhooked the prong. She unsnapped the clasp with steady fingers and pulled the zipper down past his bulging masculinity.

Instantly she found herself in the middle of his bed "Sorry, love, next time you may finish undressing me," said Dillon, leaning over her. Her sneakers were pulled off, followed by her white socks. Warm hands ran up her thighs to cup her hips. Such large hands to be so gentle. Extreme care was given to the snap of her jeans.

He bent and placed a loving kiss on the navel he'd just uncovered. With trembling fingers Dillon slowly unzipped and pulled the faded jeans off her long legs. He stood at the side of the bed and admired the picture she made in his bed. Dark hair cascaded across white sheets; eyes nearly black with passion stared at him as he kicked off his sneakers. Impatiently pulling his socks off, he gaped at the only piece of clothing she had on. A deep red triangle of silk, barely concealing her womanhood. Anxious hands pushed his jeans and underwear off in one fluid motion.

Elizabeth's eyes turned blacker with desire as she watched Dillon shed his clothes. Oh, Lord, he was superb. Cinnamon-colored hair lightly covered his broad chest. It thinned out over his flat stomach only to flair out below his navel to form a dark nest for his aroused strength. Taut thighs were lightly blanketed with the same curling cinnamon hair. Reaching for him she breathed one word, "Magnificent."

That word was the only invitation Dillon needed. Lying down next to her, he leaned over and sealed his fate forever by kissing her. Her pouting breasts brushed his chest and drove all thoughts except this loving and giving woman from his mind.

Her breath caught in her throat as his hot mouth captured one of her dusky nipples. A warm callused hand slid down her quivering stomach to gently cup the apex of her thighs. Skilled fingers slid the silky panties down her creamy thighs as he paid tribute to the other breast. Elizabeth sunk her fingers into his shoulders as his fingers climbed her inner thighs to sink deep into her moistness.

Lord, she was so warm and wet. Dillon raised his head and watched her eyes open as he withdrew his finger and plunged it back in. A delicate hand ran down his chest, flattened across his abdomen and reached for his volcanic maleness that was ready to explode at the slightest touch. He reluctantly rolled away and opened the nightstand drawer to pull out a silver packet. She watched him as he prepared himself and was glad that at least one of them was still thinking. With a shy smile she welcomed him with open arms as he settled between her thighs. His lips captured hers as he entered the sweet haven of her body. A moan sounded in the back of her throat as her body adjusted to his size.

Dillon's tentative movements caused a riot of feeling she'd never experienced before. She was wild-eyed as he bent his head and drew her erect nipple deep into his mouth. His deep thrusts matched the sucking motion of his lips. A delicious heat coiled through her when the rhythm increased, carrying her upward to a place she'd never been. Elizabeth threw back her head, arched her spine, and wrapped her legs around his powerful hips. Two more thrusts, and she reached the top of the mountain with him. "Dillon." The strangled cry emerged from her heart, as he cupped her buttocks and dove one last time into heaven.

The fading pleas of "Elizabeth" echoed off her shoulder as he tried to stifle his final cry of release.

Eight

Dillon reached for Elizabeth's soft warmth but came up empty handed. He rubbed his hand over his tired eyes; she was gone. "Damn." Pale morning light was filtering through the faded lace of his curtains. Rolling onto his side he glanced at the floor and saw that her clothes were gone too.

He buried his face in the pillow she'd used and smelled the honeysuckle fragrance of her hair. At least it hadn't been a dream; she really had been there last night. They had made incredible love, not once but twice before falling asleep in each other's arms. The first time had been quick and impatient, neither able to control the desire that sprang up between them. The second time had been glorious—slow and sensual, each exploring the other. He discovered she'd never known the feel of a man's tongue on her inner thigh; she located his ticklish spot, the soft, sensitive skin behind his knees.

So why did his lady leave? With a groan he pulled the sheets over his head and remembered three small boys sleeping down the hall. Now that would have made an interesting what-I-did-on-my-summer-vacation paper for school. Kevin and Kyle could explain how Aaron's mom had slept over and cooked breakfast. His lady had left, because she was a lady.

With the sheet blocking out the morning sun he smelled honeysuckle mixed with the scent of their lovemaking, and an instantaneous reaction occurred—arousal. With a muffled curse he pulled back the covers and headed for a cold shower.

Fifteen minutes later a whistling, damp-haired Dillon headed across his yard carrying a silver and turquoise belt and a smile. Without bothering to knock he walked into Elizabeth's kitchen and caught her making coffee. "Good morning, sunshine."

At the sound of Dillon's voice she almost lost her grip on the can of coffee. Waking up in the pale light of dawn in his arms had been magic. It felt right. The only thing that had been missing were the words *I love you*. Should she have awakened him and spoken the words her heart cried, or waited until he said them first? The faint sound of chirping birds outside had drawn her attention away from the sleeping man beside her. The kids would be waking soon and she'd better not get caught in his bed. That could take some explaining.

She had silently slipped from his warm embrace to dress hastily in wrinkled clothes. She'd wished Dillon a silent good-morning and tiptoed from his room carrying her socks and sneakers. When she'd crept home at half past five, a shower seemed the logical choice to help relieve some very sore muscles.

She smiled while standing under the warm water, thinking of all the incredible things Dillon had done to her. A blush stole up her cheeks when she recalled the things she had done to him. Was this the same woman who'd bored her ex-husband so much he divorced her? Dillon was nothing like Ron. Their love-making was as different as brussels sprouts were to cherry cheese cake: One you eat because you have to, the other because you want to savor every mouthful. She had flung a handful of wet hair out of her face and announced to all the other women in the world that they would have to find their own cherry cheese cake; this one was taken.

Towel drying her hair, she belted on an old white terry-cloth robe and strolled into the kitchen to make a pot of coffee. She was gong to need it. She had a stack of orders to fill today, with only two hours worth of sleep. Whistling "Oh, What a Beautiful Morning," she didn't hear Dillon enter the kitchen until he wished her a good-morning and practically gave her a heart attack.

"Sweet Mary, you gave me a scare."

"Sorry, love. You left this morning without something."

She looked at the belt he had laid on the table. "My belt."

With a sexy smile he grabbed her around the waist and hauled her into his arms, saying, "No, a good-morning kiss."

She felt desire rocket through her as his lips took care of this oversight. Liquid fire trailed down her stomach to the core of her soul as Dillon's tongue plunged into her willing mouth. With a slight movement of her hips she came in contact with his growing arousal. She felt a new confidence as a woman and pulled back with a chuckle. "Is this the rise in 'rise and shine'?"

Dillon gently picked her up and sat her on the counter, slowly opening the sash of her robe. Bending his head, he tenderly pulled a hardening nipple into his mouth. When he heard her moan he released the nub only to bite the other one gently. After a loving lap at the erect nipple, he straightened and smiled at the gleaming moisture. "Now you're the shine."

The speed of her reaction confused her. How could she be this responsive hours after making love to this man? Had her ex-husband lied to her? Self-contempt darkened her eyes as she thought about how cruel Ron had been when he told her how young and naive she was. Her voice held anger and loathing as she voiced her fear. "Didn't you find it boring?"

Dillon's jaw hung open as he stared at the contempt in her eyes. She thought it had been boring! In total disbelief he roared, "Boring?" They had made love into the small hours of the morning and now watching her make coffee turned him on. How could she think it was boring?

She heard Dillon's roar and blinked in further confusion.

When the woman you love and want to spend the rest of your life with thinks you are a dud in bed, there's only one thing to do—lie. Pride is such a terrible vice. He backed away from the counter, as if she had suddenly contracted the plague. He thrust out his chin, squared his shoulders, and dealt a cutting blow. "Why did you think I came over this morning?" Not bothering to wait for an answer he walked toward the door and said over his shoulder, "I was hoping by the third time we could figure out how to do it right." The slamming door punctuated the sentence.

Two steps into his yard he regretted saying it. He'd never lied to a woman before, then again he had never been told he was boring. With a disgusted sigh he kicked the peeling banister and marched into his quiet house. If he could have seen Elizabeth's face crumble as he dealt that final blow, he probably would have ripped out his own tongue.

• • • •

Elizabeth hid her puffy eyes behind a pair of sunglasses and went to make deliveries. If anyone noticed that her smile was forced and unnatural, they kept it to themselves. She did catch Aaron staring at her a couple times and vowed to try harder to act normal.

By late afternoon sweat was dripping down the valley between her breasts as she slid another cake pan into the hot oven. Aaron had gone to the pool with Dillon and his sons after Kevin had knocked on the back door to ask permission. There were no more suggestive phone calls from his father. At least Dillon was gentleman enough not to include Aaron in their argument. She would return the compliment by inviting Kevin and Kyle to the pool, even though the fatherhood lessons had obviously ended.

She moved in front of the fan and pulled the clinging top away from her damp breasts and sighed. How could she watch Kevin and Kyle and not think of their father and the one night she'd spent with him?

Dillon stood in five feet of water and demonstrated to Aaron for the third time the proper way to turn his head and breathe. Large brown eyes shone with gratitude and pleasure as the lesson paid off in the form of a twenty-foot-long uninterrupted stretch of near-perfect swimming. "That was real good, Aaron. With a little more practice you'll be swimming across the entire pool."

"Thanks, Mr. McKenzie."

Dillon watched the small boy pull himself out of the water to sit on the edge of the concrete pool. "You're welcome, but you are the one who does all the work, not me." With a morbid curiosity he asked, "So how's your mom today?"

"Okay, I guess." He paused. "She has allergies."

"Allergies?"

"Yep. Her eyes are all red and swollen. She said there must be something in the air." Aaron noticed his friends waving from the far end of the pool and stood up. "Thanks again, Mr. McKenzie."

Dillon watched as Aaron ran toward the shallow end and executed as perfect belly flop. Frustration ripped through him as he set a killer pace doing the American crawl. Two laps later he hauled his body out of the cool water. He wasn't sure what was more frustrating, trying to swim around fifty kids or figuring out why Elizabeth would be crying. With a disgusted sigh he flopped down on an old blanket and watched the boys play a game of water tag. Hell, as far as he knew, Elizabeth might have allergies.

Elizabeth kicked the sheet to the foot of her bed, mumbling a colorful curse. Nothing had gone right for the past five days. Temperatures soared into the nineties and stayed there without any relief in sight. The nights cooled down to a mere eighty-four with 70 percent humidity, and the only breeze came from electric fans or slamming doors.

Aaron started avoiding the stranger called mom and spent his days next door with his friends. A repair man was due the next morning to fix the thermostat in her oven, which had suddenly gone berserk. Orders for her baked goods slid to a halt. It was too hot to think, let alone eat. Tempers were flaring all over town, from the grocery clerk who couldn't understand how Elizabeth had gone shopping without her wallet to the road crew who had placed a dozen orange cones in the middle of the road she drove down.

She hid behind closed curtains and caught glimpses of Dillon coming or going or mowing his lawn. The man she loved washed clothes without sorting them first, served only microwaveable food, and bought a plastic wading pool for Rufus. The man she loved thought she was boring. How could the most significant night of her life be considered boring? Dillon obviously didn't feel the same ecstasy in her arms as she did from his lightest touch. Tears stung her eyes as she stared up at the darkened ceiling. How was she ever going to live next door to Dillon without going quietly out of her mind?

She was going to take control of her life! It wasn't fair to Aaron to have a deranged lunatic for a mother. The fatherhood lessons Dillon had given her would have to be enough; there weren't going to be anymore. With determination she thought of the final exam: a camping trip. A smile curved her lips as she imagined Aaron's excitement when she gave him the news. Monday they were leaving on a five-day camping trip to the mountains. She'd take the final without Dillon's help.

With that resolved she turned over onto her stomach and brushed her long dark hair away from her back. Perspiration lightly covered her body as she bunched the pillow into a deformed lump and prayed for sleep.

To the man silently sitting on well-worn steps of the wooden veranda, sleep wouldn't come. For the twelfth time that night Dillon mentally replayed the final scene in Elizabeth's kitchen. She didn't actually say making love had been boring; she asked if he thought it was. Staring over at her house shrouded in darkness, he wondered what possessed her to ask such a degrading question?

Had he acted bored? Remembering the smell of honeysuckle and the sweet taste of her lips sent a low hum of desire down his spine. He cursed his overactive imagination and leaned back on his elbows, gazing up at the stars. The most profound experience in his life was making love to Elizabeth. The emotional aspects scared the hell out of him. It was like coming home. The physical act was more than a joining; it was a merger of body and soul. Hell, the woman he loved thought that was boring.

Aaron had practically moved into his house. A smile curved his lips as he pictured Aaron, covered head to toe in mud, holding a turtle. With amusement he had shoved Aaron into the bathtub and washed every stitch of clothing he had on, including his once red sneakers. Bubba, the turtle, had found a home in the bathroom sink while Aaron, dressed in Kyle's clothes, had called home to ask if he could eat dinner with Kevin and Kyle. After dinner, Aaron had dressed back into his own, now-dried clothes. Dillon had sat on the couch drying Aaron's sneakers with Rachael's old blow-dryer, as the boy said a tearful farewell to Bubba and gave Kevin and Kyle instructions on how to take care of him. Aaron had pleaded with Dillon not to tell his mom about Bubba, stating she wouldn't understand. Dillon knew she would, but the boy was obviously upset. What harm was there in harboring a boxer turtle?

Dillon smiled as he remembered the morning he took Bubba in. He had been awakened by hysterical cries from Kevin and Kyle; Bubba had escaped his cardboard box in the bathroom sometime during the night. For the next two hours, three males dressed only in underwear had searched for the fugitive. They'd finally found him snuggled deep in his shell, hiding under a dirty shirt Kevin had thrown in the corner of his bedroom. New rules on Bubba had been negotiated when Aaron came over later that morning. Obviously Bubba hadn't liked being confined to a cardboard box.

Three against one weren't fair odds to begin with, but the huge tears in dark eyes that were just like his mother's had clinched it. Dillon would have signed the house over to Bubba to stop Aaron's tears. The entire bathroom became Bubba's.

The boys didn't seem to mind stepping over Bubba every time they used the bathroom. And the turtle loved playing in the sinkful of water and taking showers with Kevin. Aaron spent every available moment with his pet. Never one to miss an opportunity, Dillon casually asked questions about his mother.

He'd learned that Elizabeth still had an allergy problem and had started doing "really dumb stuff," as Aaron put it. Aaron had relayed the story of her driving over a dozen plastic orange cones. When the guy in the hard hat had asked if she'd gotten her driver's license in a Cracker Jack box, she called him a moron. Then she'd told him to go home and play Legos before some innocent driver got hurt. With morbid curiosity Dillon had grilled Aaron as to what happened next and wasn't surprised to hear her allergies had started acting up again.

The whole thing wasn't making sense anymore. If she really thought making love with him was boring, why would she be acting strange and crying all the time now that he was out of her life? Dillon heaved a deep sigh and stood up to stretch. He headed back into his study to catch up on some work.

"Aaron, slow down. You're going to choke on your breakfast." With an amused glance she watched her son take a deep breath and continue eating his French toast at a more leisurely pace. She took a sip of coffee and smiled. "How would you like to go on a vacation?"

Startled brown eyes looked up from his plate. "With who?"

"Me, silly."

"Where?"

"Camping in the Blue Ridge Mountains of Virginia."

"Why?"

"What's this twenty questions?" A frown pulled at her mouth. "You don't sound very excited about this."

How would he explain about Bubba? Dillon had made the turtle his responsibility. He didn't want to leave his new friends, but he'd never been camping before. "Can Kevin, Kyle, and Dillon come with us?"

Blinking back tears, she said, "No, Aaron. It will just be you, me, and Mother Nature."

Seeing the sadness in his mother's eyes confused him. "Will we be sleeping in a tent and cooking on a fire?"

She forced a smile. "Yes, we can borrow a tent and sleeping bags from Rosa and Mario's son Tony."

"When are we leaving?"

"Monday morning, bright and early." Uncertainty and confusion clouded her son's face. "Don't you want to go?"

Aaron downed the remaining milk in his glass before answering, "Sure, Mom, it will be great." He jumped from his seat and planted a kiss on his mother's cheek as he headed out the back door. "I'm going over to Kyle's to tell him."

Elizabeth sat and stared at her son's half-eaten breakfast. For the first time she could remember, he hadn't carried his plate over to the sink. He'd also left the table without being excused and ran next door without asking permission. With a shake of her head she cleared the table and decided

Aaron really must be excited about the camping trip.

Dillon came out of his study for another cup of coffee and spotted Aaron sitting on his couch with Bubba in his lap. "Hi, Aaron."

"Good morning, Mr. McKenzie."

A person would have to be blind not to notice the dejected look on Aaron's face. "Something bothering you, son?" he asked as he sat down next to him. He watched as Aaron gently stroked the wrinkled bald head of Bubba. If he didn't know any better he would have sworn the damn turtle smiled.

"Can you please watch Bubba for a few days for me?"

"Why?"

"My mother is acting strange again."

Dillon's heart skipped a beat before asking, "How?" He silently prayed Aaron wouldn't say she was crying again because there was no way he could ignore it any longer. He was gong over there to find out what she was allergic to.

"We are going camping."

Dillon's voice squeaked as he asked, "With whom?"

"Me, mom, and Mother Nature."

He took a deep breath to calm his heart. "Has your mother ever gone camping before?"

Aaron gave Dillon a look that clearly indicated Dillon was also losing his mind. "No, she won't even sit on the porch at night because the mosquitoes drive her nuts. Last year she wouldn't even let me watch *Wild America* because she was scared I'd have nightmares."

Dillon knew what was happening; she was taking her final exam without him, or at least she thought so. There was no way he was going to let her strap on a backpack and drag a seven-year-old boy into God's country. "When are you going?"

"Monday morning."

"Do you know where you're camping?"

"Virginia. Someplace called Blue Mountain."

"Blue Ridge Mountains?"

"Yeah, that's it."

Oh, Lord, it was worse than he thought. She was camping in bear country. Scenes from the movie he'd rented flashed through his mind. He forced a gentle smile, ruffled Aaron's hair, and lied. "No problem, son. Me and the boys will look after Bubba. Do you know how long you're going for?"

He saw the negative shake of Aaron's head and probed, "Are you staying on Skyline Drive?"

"What's that?"

"It's a road over a hundred miles long that runs right across the top of the Blue Ridge Mountains. It has a couple of campsites, hiking trails, and information centers. If that's where you are staying, I've been there before. I could tell you what to look for."

"Thanks, Mr. McKenzie. I'll try to find out."

Guilt descended on his shoulders for tricking a child, but he was getting desperate. He walked toward the kitchen and the full coffee pot. He had a lot of work to get through before Monday.

"Hey, Dad, can I ask you a question?"

Dillon looked at his eldest son, Kevin, and groaned. He was only nine years old, too young for the facts of life. In his nine years of being a parent he had learned one thing: Whenever a child started a conversation like this, it meant trouble. "Sure, son."

"Do you like Mrs. Lancaster?"

A tentative smile broke across his mouth as he looked at his son. "How would you feel about it if I said yes."

Kevin shrugged his shoulders and answered, "Okay, I guess."

"I mean really like her," added Dillon.

After a long, serious look at his father, Kevin asked, "As in kissing and all that junk?"

Dillon suppressed the laugh threatening to erupt at the thought of "all that junk." "Yes, that kind of liking."

Kevin's freckles wiggled as he smiled and said, "That's good. Uncle Shane says a man shouldn't be without a woman. Me and Kyle were starting to worry about you."

With an incredulous look, Dillon asked, "When did Shane tell you that?"

"The day he helped us move in."

He needed to know but was hesitant to ask the next question. "What else did Shane say?"

"Something about giving you room to operate. But you're not a doctor, so I didn't know what that meant."

Dillon ran his fingers through his hair and groaned. "Can you please forget everything Uncle Shane told you?" He watched his son nod his head and asked, "Do you like Mrs. Lancaster and Aaron?"

"Aaron's okay, even if he is younger than me. And Mrs. Lancaster is the greatest. I told her I liked walnuts and she promised to put some in the next batch of chocolate chip cookies she bakes." A curious look came over Kevin as he looked at his father. "If you like Mrs. Lancaster, how come she never comes over anymore?"

"A slight misunderstanding. But don't worry. We're about to clear it up." Dillon ruffled his son's hair and headed out the kitchen before Kevin could ask any more questions that he might not be able to answer.

• • •

Elizabeth pulled off her sunglasses and stared at her deserted campsite. Leaves and twigs were scattered across the packed dirt. Barely a blade of grass had survived peak tourist season. A scarred picnic table sat by a pile of black ashes. Her eyes traveled to the woods surrounding her secluded campsite, and she shivered.

She looked around at the empty site next to theirs and realized they were virtually alone. Should she go back to the extremely hassled girl at the check-in point and request another site, one closer to humanity? Her gaze fell on the hand-sketched map of the camp the girl had handed her and noticed she wasn't far away from fellow campers. In fact, right through that clump of bushes were sites fifty-six to sixty. One good scream would bring someone running, and with any luck someone would pull into the empty site next to hers.

"Well, how does it look?"

Aaron looked around and grinned. "Neat, Mom. Do you think there really are bears around here like the ranger said?"

In one quick movement Elizabeth was out of the car before Aaron noticed the effect his question had caused: terror. "No! Come on, you have to help me set up the tent and gather wood for our fire."

She inserted the key into her trunk and stood back as it sprang open. Things didn't look too squashed, considering she'd had to sit on the trunk lid to close it. Elizabeth grabbed two folding chairs and leaned them against the rear bumper. She reached into the trunk and unloaded two boxes filled with pots, pans, bowls, and assorted cooking paraphernalia. Next came the propane stove, the lantern, and a spare can of fuel. Flashlights tumbled to the ground as she hauled out the tent and carried it over to the spot she deemed fit. Aaron helped carry over the poles, stakes, and a hammer. The pioneering spirit seeped into Elizabeth and Aaron as they worked diligently to pitch their tent. Poles were raised; stakes were pounded. Poles were lowered, switched around, and hoisted again in different order. By the third time Elizabeth declared the tent was perfect, even though it did tilt to the left.

After dusting her hands on the back of her jeans she opened the back door of her car and caught Aaron's pillow before it hit the ground. Pillows, sleeping bags, and suitcases were hauled into the tent, along with two comforters and a spare pillow. She gave Aaron the job of finding the red plastic tablecover while she tried to unbury the cooler from the back seat, so she could add the ice she had purchased at the camp store.

Elizabeth handed Aaron a container of cold fruit juice and opened a book on the snakes of North America. Twenty minutes later she was an expert on which snakes to avoid—all of them. "Are you ready to help me collect firewood so we can roast marshmallows tonight?"

"Sure, Mom. I'll get the ax."

A smile curved her lips as her son raced to the car. "Not the ax, bring the hatchet. I'll get the camera."

Half an hour later Elizabeth found herself deep in the woods with enough wood stacked around her to last a week. "I think we have plenty of wood, Aaron." Silently she added, *Now if I can only remember the way back to the camp.* She threaded the hatchet through her belt loop and grabbed two of the biggest branches, then started toward camp.

"Where you going, Mom?"

"Back to camp, honey."

A concerned look came to Aaron's eyes. "That's the wrong way."

Elizabeth dropped her burden and did a one-hundred-and-eighty-degree turn, thinking it all looked the same—trees, leaves, and strange rustlings. The compass was in the car along with the book on how to navigate by the stars. They were lost. She kept her face expressionless so she wouldn't panic Aaron. "Oh, yeah, smarty pants, then which way do we go?"

Without any hesitation he pointed to his right. "That way."

She watched as he picked up two branches and dragged them the way he had just pointed. With a shrug of her shoulders she bent over to pick up her branches when the hatchet slipped through the loop and landed on her toe. A muffled curse escaped her lips. But she sent a prayer heavenward, grateful that the sharp blade hadn't hit first. Elizabeth limped as she dragged her branches after her son, toward an unknown destination.

Fifteen minutes later they stared in awe as three deer grazed in a clearing. With her fingers to her lips Elizabeth signaled to Aaron to lower his branches and follow her. Mother and son quietly crept closer to the animals. Thirty yards away, hiding behind a tree, Elizabeth positioned the camera and snapped a picture. Three frightened deer stared at them before running in the opposite direction. A second picture was taken of hind legs and white fluffy tails. "I didn't mean to scare them off."

Aaron whispered. "They looked like Bambi."

She wiped at a smear of dirt on his cheek. "I'm sure we will see some more animals. Let's get back to camp. It's almost time to start dinner. After we eat, it's hit the showers, then marshmallows and bed. Tomorrow we'll wake up early and find one of those hiking trails Dillon told you about."

Ten minutes later two weary adventurers limped into camp dragging their firewood behind them.

With more determination than skill Elizabeth started to chop at the branch with her hatchet, while Aaron looked for kindling. Perspiration made her back itch, and a blister was forming on her right hand when mosquitoes attacked.

Elizabeth pressed her hands to the small of her back and gave up wood chopping for the night. Aaron could eat his marshmallows raw for one night. She grabbed a first-aid kit from the back seat that would have made a paramedic in New York City proud, and then removed a can of insect repellent. Aaron was the first to be sprayed with the foul-smelling ointment. After he was declared bugproof she sprayed her forearms and smeared some on her face and neck. She forced a smile for her son and prayed for darkness and a comfortable sleeping bag. She had been up since five, and driving six hours straight wasn't her idea of fun. Her toe throbbed, her blister burned, and she smelled like a toxic waste dump.

"Is it dinnertime yet, Mom? I'm hungry."

"Sure, honey. Help me set up the stove and we'll be in business."

Aaron struggled to carry over two boxes filled with food, while she rummaged around looking for matches. She set the green stove on the end of the picnic table and followed the instructions to the letter. Open the lid and set the wind barriers in place. Pump the little handle, turn the knob, and light the burner. So simple an elementary-school student could do it, Tony had said. After the third try and two burned fingers she would have given Aaron the matches if she wasn't scared to death the stove would blow up.

The pump wouldn't move any more, and the valve hissed as she turned it. Lighting the entire book of matches she set off a chain of events unequaled in the history of the Shenandoah Valley.

Elizabeth jumped back as a huge ball of flames

bellowed into the air above the stove. She lost her balance as she tripped over the branch she had been hacking and landed butt first on their tent. Poles collapsed around her as she stared at the wisp of black smoke that once was an angry, blazing ball of flames.

Dillon drove around the secluded clump of trees to witness her idea of outdoor cooking and felt his hair turn gray. He slammed on the brakes and raced from the van. He threw a pan of soapy water on Elizabeth's melting table cloth. With extreme care he turned off the stove. Then turning to the woman sitting in a pile of blue canvas, he roared, his voice as black as night, "What in the hell are you trying to do, kill yourself?"

Elizabeth slowly came out of her daze and looked at the mountain of a man standing in front of her. Tears of confusion, gratitude, and love filled her eyes as she whispered, "Dillon."

Nine

Elizabeth melted into Dillon's arms as he hauled her up. With safe arms tenderly surrounding her and the events of the past week pressing on her mind, she asked the question burning in her heart, "Am I boring?"

Dillon threw back his head and laughed. Desperately trying to catch his breath, he said, "Boring? Any minute I expect to see smoke jumpers parachuting in, and you think you're boring?"

She snuggled deeper into his embrace and whispered, "That's not what I mean."

With a gentle hand he lifted her dirt-smeared face and looked into her eyes. "I love you." Placing a swift kiss on her surprised mouth, he added, "Tonight after the boys are settled, we have a lot to talk about."

For the first time Elizabeth realized they weren't alone. Kevin, Kyle, and Aaron were running around the campsite gesturing wildly at the stove and the woods beyond. Listening to Aaron tell about the deer they had seen earlier, she smiled. "What are you and the boys doing here?"

"By the look of things, saving the Blue Ridge

Mountains." He saw her raised eyebrow and smiled. "You can't take a final exam without the teacher to grade you."

She stepped out of his arms. "I think I might have to cheat on this one."

"Cheating's not allowed, but I can be bribed."

A seductive light shone in her eyes as she asked, "With what?"

After a quick glance at the boys, he reluctantly replied, "For now I'll settle for dinner."

A look of dismay crossed her face as she glanced around the campsite. Dillon must really think she was totally incompetent. Her neat blue tent lay in a wrinkled lump, the stove was sitting in a puddle of suds, and boxes of food were soaking up excess water. The trunk of her car was open to reveal a tangled mass of boxes, bags, and assorted camping equipment. The folding chairs lay on the ground next to a two-foot-high pile of kindling. "Do you really want me to cook dinner?"

Dillon's eyes sparkled as he looked around. At six o'clock this morning he'd watched, from behind closed curtains, as she had loaded the car. Laughter had vibrated from his chest as he witnessed her sitting on the trunk of her car until it locked. In total amazement he then watched as she jammed a cooler, suitcases, pillows, and books into the back seat, barely managing to close the door. A smile had curved his mouth as he finished his coffee, watching Elizabeth and Aaron, armed with a stack of road maps, back out of the driveway.

His Elizabeth had guts. She was taking Aaron camping alone, in bear country. With a grimace he wondered if she even knew black bears still roamed the Blue Ridge Mountains. A sense of urgency had come over him as he mounted the stairs to wake his sons. They were going camping.

As he stood a foot away from Elizabeth he marveled at how beautiful she looked covered with dirt, leaves, and pieces of bark. Lovingly placing a kiss on the end of her nose, he said, "Sure I want you to cook. There's a trick to these stoves, and I'm going to show it to you." Gently propelling her back toward the table, he asked, "By the way, what's for dinner?"

"Yeah, Mrs. Lancaster, what's for dinner? We're starved."

Laughter bubbled up for the first time in days. "Kevin, you are always hungry." Smiling at Dillon, she said, "You guys have a choice of hotdogs or stew."

Three boys voted unanimously for hotdogs, while Dillon chose the stew. With help from Kevin she cleaned up the table and dug through the boxes for dinner. They decided to store the food in Elizabeth's car so the bears couldn't reach it. By the time they were ready for Dillon's help to light the stove, his tent was pitched and he had started sorting out hers.

Dinner was cooked without any further disasters, and they all gathered around her table to eat. "Hey, Dad, can Aaron sleep in our tent with us?"

"Sure, but don't you think Elizabeth will be lonely?"

In youthful innocence Kyle declared. "You can sleep in her tent with her, Dad."

Elizabeth felt the buttermilk biscuit stick in her throat, and she started to choke. One good whack on her back from Dillon left her gasping for breath.

"You boys don't want me sleeping in there with you?"

"Ah, Dad, we don't need you."

Not liking the way the conversation was heading, Elizabeth raised a disapproving eyebrow at Dillon. A glint of mischief sparkled in his green eyes as he said, "How about if you boys take our tent, I'll sleep in Aaron's tent, and we'll let Elizabeth sleep in the back of the van?"

"Great."

"Neat."

"Okay."

"Elizabeth?"

Love and excitement shone in her eyes. He'd planned that. He was giving them the time to be alone they desperately needed. In a voice raw with emotion only Dillon would understand, she mumbled, "Sounds great to me."

As they finished dinner Dillon explained about the hiking trail they would be tackling the next day. Dishes were washed and packed away. The tent Dillon would use was set up, and sleeping bags were put in order. As the sunlight quickly faded, they all headed for the showers.

Twenty minutes later a shivering Elizabeth pushed her way out of the ladies' room. Damp hair streamed down the back of her soft, pink sweat suit. She spotted Dillon sitting by a tree waiting for her and smiled. "Do you know they don't have any hot water?"

He rose slowly to his feet holding his bundle of dirty clothes and a towel. "I know. All they have is one setting: ice-cold." With a tender kiss across her lips he took the tote bag she was clutching. "It didn't help. I still want you."

A blush crept up her cheeks. The shivering was replaced by a burning heat. "The feeling's mutual."

Dillon placed the tote bag over his shoulder, clasped her hand, and gently led her out from under the fluorescent lights and into the twilight surrounding their camp. "I sent the boys back already. They're supposed to be finding green sticks for roasting the marshmallows."

"I have some hot chocolate, somewhere."

"Honey, I think you packed your entire kitchen and jammed it in your car." He chuckled.

"Humph. Remember who supplied dinner to-night."

Darkness fell over the campers and with it came the hiss of propane lanterns and the crackling of fires. The boys were stuffed with burnt, gooey marshmallows and had climbed into their sleeping bags. Elizabeth and Dillon sat close together in front of the dying fire. "Do you think they'll be okay?" she asked, as the flashlight beams played against the sides of the boys' tent.

Dillon lightly caressed the beating pulse in Elizabeth's small wrist. He smiled at the boys playing with their flashlights under their sleeping bags, and said, "No bear in his right mind will go up against those boys."

Her teeth sunk into her lower lip as visions of the grizzly attacking the blond coed came to mind. "I'm serious, Dillon."

He took her small trembling hand and pressed it between his two warm palms. "I know you are, love. Bears won't attack a tent unless it smells food and is extremely hungry. I'll be sleeping in the other tent not fifteen feet away. Bears aren't known for their quietness."

He felt her relax and placed her hand back onto her own chair. "I'll get us another cup of coffee and build up the fire. If you stay in the smoke, it will keep the mosquitoes off," he mentioned as she swatted an insect.

Elizabeth moved the chairs a few inches closer to the smoke and watched as he poured coffee from the pot sitting on a rock near the flames. The pot was Dillon's, and by the look of it, it had seen combat. It was dented, blackened beyond scouring, and made the most delicious cup of coffee she'd ever tasted. In fascination she watched the firelight play over his features as he added a few more logs.

As he sat down and handed her a cup he knew

the time had come. "I seem to have gotten lost somewhere in our relationship. I think I followed it pretty good until your comment about being bored." He cleared the lump forming in his throat, and said, "I still don't know if you meant I was boring, you were boring, or if we were boring together." Sensing she was about to comment, he quickly continued. "Before you say anything, I would like to apologize for that last statement I made. My only excuse is I was upset and totally irrational at that moment. The woman I love and had made incredible love with all night told me I was boring or something to that effect. I'm not sure anymore what you said, or what you meant. I would appreciate it if you would start at the beginning and try to explain."

Elizabeth sat in stunned silence as Dillon explained how he felt. No one had ever bared their soul to her before. It had some dire ramifications: she must bare hers in return. She stared into the orange-and-blue flames and gathered her courage to open her heart. "I was twenty-one when I met Ron. He was good looking, charming, and a ladies' man. Within five months we were married."

Raising the coffee to her lips she wished it was something stronger. When Dillon didn't comment she continued. "I was a virgin on our wedding night. That was probably the main attraction to him. I wouldn't sleep with him before the wedding, so I guess I was a challenge."

Dillon forced his hand to relax on the ceramic mug he held. In a sympathetic voice he asked, "Rough night?"

"Not really. The first week he was the perfect husband. He understood the shyness and uncertainty that I was feeling. By the end of the second week, things started to slide. At the end of the month it hit rock bottom. That's when the name-calling started."

"What kind of names?"

"Frigid, boring, the usual stuff that any naive twenty-one-year-old believes. I started going to the library and reading anything I could find on the subject of sex. I even tried a couple of their suggestions.

When Elizabeth fell silent he asked, "What happened?"

A laugh somewhere between humor and disgust escaped her lips. "I was laughed at and called more degrading names. Ron started spending several nights in a row away from home. Then I found out I was pregnant."

Dillon caught the subtle movement of her hand across her stomach and the genuine smile before it disappeared. "Silly me, I thought it would make some difference." A grunt that could have been a chuckle sounded. "Ah, it did make a difference. Ron stopped coming home all together, and I spent six hours a day in the bathroom being sick.

"Our marriage lasted six months. He showed up one day with some blonde, barely out of high school, and said he wanted a divorce. His parting shot was, 'You're as boring as a G-rated movie.' "

Elizabeth finished the remainder of her coffee in one gulp. "The other morning I was remembering all those names and wondering if you thought I was boring. I never thought you were boring. Our love-making was the most fantastic experience in my life. I'm sorry you misunderstood. I never meant to hurt you."

He knew she had guts, and this just proved it, in spades. She'd opened up all those old wounds and took a chance on him. With love and time he hoped to heal them for good. "First question. Is that bastard still alive?"

She chuckled softly. "I don't know or care. I haven't heard from Ron in almost eight years."

"The feelings we shared the other night, did

you ever experience them with Ron or anyone else?"

Eyes wide with incredibility turned and stared at Dillon. "Are you out of your mind? There hasn't been anyone since Ron, and I don't think I want to compare what I felt the other night, in your arms, to anything with Ron."

Dillon released the breath he hadn't realized he was holding. "I love you, Elizabeth Lancaster."

She looked over at the boys' quiet tent and figured they were asleep. Slowly rising to her feet she picked up the blackened coffee pot and dumped the liquid on the dying embers. With great care she folded her chair and leaned it against a tree.

Dillon was fascinated as she grabbed the bottom of her sweat shirt and pulled it over her head. He stared at the faint outline of her breasts against a sleeveless T-shirt. "What are you doing?" he asked hoarsely.

Her voice was a low, intimate caress. "I'm going to show you how much I love you, Dillon James McKenzie. Words aren't enough."

Not one of his muscles moved as she bent and went inside his tent. The closing of the flap propelled him into motion. His chair ended up against hers. He doused the embers again, then checked the vehicles. A quick glance around the site showed everything in order and bearproof.

He entered the tent and zipped the flap shut behind him. Elizabeth was sitting on his sleeping bag. The sound of her clothes being removed caught his attention. "What, no lights?"

The sound of her soft, feminine purr slid down his spine. "I heard that if you turn lights on inside a tent it silhouettes everything against the canvas." The word canvas was muffled by her T-shirt going over her head. "And what I plan on doing to you, Mr. McKenzie, would get us arrested."

With trembling fingers he pulled his shirt over his head and drew off his sneakers and socks. Sitting on the edge of his sleeping bag he realized that she had unzipped and opened it up. In hurried movements he peeled off his jeans and found the silver packet in their pocket.

He ran his hands across the flannel and encountered a slim, smooth ankle. A smile curved his lips. It was a wonderful place to start.

Elizabeth felt the warmth of Dillon's palm on her leg. "I'm the one who is supposed to be showing how much I love you."

His voice was harsh with desire. "If you so much as touch me now, it will be over." He slid his palm up her calf and whispered, "Do you know how exciting it was knowing you were undressing and I couldn't see you?"

She felt a string of feather-soft kisses up her shin bone and sighed. "I think I should be insulted by that remark."

In the total blackness he chuckled, and said, "So far, I found you have removed your shoes, socks, and sweatpants. I'm pretty sure you took off that sexy T-shirt." As he lifted his lips from the back of her knee, he questioned, "When did they start making T-shirts like that? I must be behind on women's apparel." He bent and kissed the other knee before asking, "The question burning in my mind is, did you take off your panties?"

She felt the warmth of his hands, the lightness of his lips, and sighed. "There's only one way to find out." Her heart raced as his gentle hands slid up her thighs, tenderly caressing the satin skin over her hips and resting lightly on her waist. Desperate hands clutched at his shoulders and drew his mouth up to her waiting lips.

A moan resounded deep in her throat as his tongue plunged into the sweet depth of her mouth. Soft, full breasts cushioned his hard chest as he wound her hair around his fist. Elizabeth entwined her arms around his neck and pulled him closer.

Dillon dragged his mouth away from the sweet torture of her lips and nibbled playfully at her ear lobe. "Say it."

She trailed her fingernails down his spine, feeling him shiver, and said, "I want you." A light nip at her ear reprimanded her. "I need you." The next nip was accompanied by a growl. She raised her hands, gently bracketing his face, and whispered, "I love you."

In the next instant all playfulness vanished from their love-making. Dillon's mouth didn't coax or request a response, it demanded one. She answered in total abandonment. Mouths seared, hands searched, and her hips rose in a rhythm as ancient as Eve's.

With trembling hands he quickly prepared himself and positioned himself at the portal of heaven. His breath was coming in hurried gasps as he placed kisses over her eyes, nose, and cheekbones. Her small hands gripped his buttocks, in an attempt to hurry him home, and sent him over the edge. His voice was harsh with the truth as he whispered, "I love you," thrusting forward and sealing her lips with his.

Warm, silky thighs cradled his hips, and feminine heels dug into the back of his knees. In a hopeless attempt to slow things down, he released her warm mouth and trailed a string of kisses down her arched throat. He was ready to explode when he sensed she had reached the summit. A plea escaped her lips—"Dillon"—as she catapulted over the edge. Two thrusts later he joined her in the explosion that shook their bodies.

Elizabeth raised her head from the nicest pillow she'd ever had—Dillon's chest. "Did I thank you for following us to Virginia?"

A chuckle shook his chest as he stated, "If you thank me any more, I'll be dead." With a gentle hand he motioned her head back onto his shoulder. "You aren't mad that we followed?"

She felt his fingers tenderly stroking her hair. "No, I'm glad you're here." Purposely she put authority into her voice. "Aaron and I could have handled this camping trip without your help. So don't get all macho on me."

Dillon placed a kiss on her forehead and smiled. "I promise not to get macho. You and Aaron had everything under control, except, maybe, the stove. But you handled that like a pro at dinner, so I guess it's safe to assume you are going to pass your final."

A mischievous smile tilted up the corners of her mouth as she turned her head and kissed his collar bone. Why hadn't she realized how sensual his collar bone was before? "Are you still grading me?" she questioned, as his arms contracted around her.

Dillon felt her angel-soft kisses across his chest and arousal stirred. Would he ever get enough of this woman? "Keep that up and I might change your C average."

A light nibble at his nipples buried under soft hair had him sucking in oxygen. "You're working on a C-plus." A moist tongue circled his navel and his voice deepened. "Definitely B material."

Her soft, full breasts brushed his thigh while silky threads of hair whispered across his scalding skin. Heat pounded in his body as he tried sitting up, pleading, "Elizabeth, come here."

Gently pushing his chest back down to its former position with one hand, she softly ran her fingers up the sensitive inside of his thigh. "I told you I want to show you how much I love you. Lie back and enjoy. I promise I won't hurt you."

With sure strokes and gentle caresses she brought

him to his full masculine glory. In a move that had Dillon breathless, she straddled his hips and took him home. A slow, even rocking of her hips had his hands clinching her waist. Slightly increasing the pace she threw back her head and arched her back.

The harsh breathing was the only sound in the tent as Dillon slid his hands up to cup her pouting breasts. He sunk his teeth into his lip to gain some control and then gently rolled the pert nipples between his thumb and forefinger. A shudder went down his spine as she moaned his name and escalated the tempo.

He felt her climax cresting, gripped her hips to keep the rhythm going as she convulsed around him and joined him in ecstasy.

The mountain air was cool as he pulled the comforter over them, and she snuggled deeper into his warmth. "I have to get to the van," was yawned into his shoulder.

"Shhh. I'll get you there before the boys wake up." Tenderly he tucked the blanket around her shoulder and asked, "Stay with me?"

One word was whispered into the blackness before sleep overtook her—"Always."

"Yuk, Dad, that looks gross."

"Gee, Mr. McKenzie, my mom's eggs never looked like that. Maybe we should wake her up."

Dillon looked at the burned, runny mess in the blackened frying pan and had to agree—it was disgusting. A curious glance at the van showed no movement from within. Sleeping Beauty slumbered on and the Prince was about to poison the troops. "Sorry, Aaron, but we're going to let your mom sleep." His gaze fell back on the smoking frying pan. "Did your mom pack any cereal?"

"Yes, sir."

A smile touched Dillon's mouth. "You may call me Mr. McKenzie or Dillon, but please don't call me sir." He saw the hesitant look on Aaron's face and quickly added, "It makes me feel old."

The smile that broke across Aaron's face showed a large gap where his front teeth once were. "Thanks—, Mr. McKenzie. I'll get the cereal."

The boys and Dillon were just about done with their breakfast when Elizabeth emerged from the van. Dressed in the wrinkled, pink sweat suit from the previous night and with a wild mass of tangled hair, she was a sight to behold. Flushed cheeks and sleep-laden eyes stared at Dillon and the boys, then at the sun just rising over the farthest ridge. She brushed back a strand of hair caught in the early morning breeze and took a step forward, landed on a sharp twig, and uttered one word, "Coffee."

Dillon suppressed a smile and quickly did her bidding. He watched, fascinated, as she slowly made her way to the picnic table, sat, and downed the hot liquid. Amusement lifted his brow as she handed him an empty cup and whispered, "More please."

He refilled her cup and chuckled. Elizabeth Lancaster, perfect mother and a four-star chef, was not a morning person. His smile faded as he stared down at his cereal bowl and scowled.

Elizabeth leisurely drank the second cup of coffee and looked around to get her bearings. Looking like something out of a horror show, she was sitting at a picnic table having coffee with Dillon and their sons. Lifting a hand, she tried to comb her fingers through her hair but they got tangled and wouldn't budge. The boys were busy poring over a guide book she had purchased the previous day, deciding which trail would be the best. Dillon was glaring at his cereal as she asked, "Is there something wrong with the cereal?"

"Ah, no."

As he lifted a spoonful, frowned at it, and placed it back in his bowl, she asked, "Dillon, don't you like the cereal?"

Dejectedly, he muttered, "It was the only thing left. The boys ate all the Cocoa Puffs."

She bit the inside of her cheek to keep from laughing. "Eat it anyway. It's good for you. It has no preservatives, no cholesterol, no sugar, and no salt."

"You forgot one: no taste."

She kept a straight face and said, "It has fiber, protein, and ten essential vitamins."

"It looks like hamster food."

Elizabeth couldn't hold it in any longer; she burst out laughing. When Dillon and the boys joined in, a feeling of rightness came over her. They were acting like a family. Wonder, joy, and love shone in her eyes as she smiled at Dillon. "I'll cook you breakfast if you chop the wood for tonight's fire?"

A deal was quickly reached and breakfast was cooked. With a completely innocent look on her face she leaned toward Dillon and whispered, "How come I don't have any panties on?"

A red-faced Dillon stopped chomping on his eggs and bacon long enough to glare at her. The message was clear: paybacks are hell.

"That's it. I cannot climb, walk, or crawl one more inch. You guys go on without me; just pick up my bones on the way back."

Dillon shifted the backpack and glanced over his shoulder at Elizabeth, as she collapsed on the nearest log. Smiling gently he took in her flushed face and heavy breathing. The trail was more difficult than he had thought, but the boys insisted this was the one. His eyes sparked with admiration at the boys' stamina. Aaron and Kyle were leaning against a huge tree, while Kevin sat in the middle of the path. Not one complaint had escaped their lips on the strenuous journey uphill. It was a private challenge among the boys as to which one would be the first to give up. None of them wanted to lose. If only the same could be said for Elizabeth. "Come on. We're almost there."

Still struggling for air, she gasped, "You said that three miles ago."

"It was more like three minutes ago." He watched the determined look on her face and asked, "You want to see the hawks don't you? Isn't that why you packed your camera?"

Elizabeth leaned her head back and gazed up between towering pines at the blue sky. She did notice a large bird circling. "Dillon, love, I hate to break this to you but they are not hawks. They're vultures waiting for the meaty flesh of any poor hiker who doesn't make it to the top of this mountain."

"Sick, Elizabeth."

With a show of pure dramatics she beseeched, "Go quickly, save yourselves. I'll sacrifice this weary body so that my dream may live." After delivering this speech she clutched her chest and fell backward into a soft bed of ferns.

As Dillon retraced his steps toward Elizabeth he smiled at Aaron. "Don't worry, son, the air thins out up this high and affects some people this way."

Forty-five minutes later Dillon sat next to the woman he'd coaxed, pleaded, and half-dragged up the mountain. The magnificent view was breathtaking. The valley was lined with a patchwork quilt of farms thousands of feet below, and fluffy white clouds were practically within reach. In the distance, ribbon-thin roads threaded their way across valleys and through the rolling countryside. Majestic hawks circled and dipped, at home in the heavens. He saw the awestruck expression on Elizabeth's face and asked, "Now aren't you glad you came?"

She lowered her camera to her lap and mumbled, "No," then spoiled it by laughing. "It's like being in heaven," she said, placing a light kiss on his tanned cheek. "Thank you for bringing me."

Dillon looked over his shoulder at the boys eating their lunch and watching the circling hawks. It wasn't the right time or place but he couldn't wait any longer. With trembling fingers he gently cupped her cheeks. "Do you remember the fog we walked through when we'd just about reached the top?"

She sensed the seriousness of the question and replied honestly, "Yes. I asked you about it and you mumbled something about San Francisco."

Green eyes burned with an intensity she'd never seen before. "It wasn't fog. We walked through a cloud."

Excitement and wonder brightened her face as she said, "Then we are in heaven."

With love in his eyes and voice, he said, "Yes, we are in heaven. I walked you right up to heaven's gate to ask you."

Elizabeth's heart rate tripled. Her hands shook as she placed them on over his. "Ask me what?"

In a voice harsh with emotion, he asked, "Will you do me the honor of becoming my wife?"

Ten

"Wife?"

"Marriage, hitched, matrimony. You know, the big step." Amusement sparkled in his eyes.

"Oh, my."

"Wrong answer, sweetheart. Say 'Oh, yes.' "

Elizabeth slowly lowered her trembling hands to her lap. She glanced toward the boys. They had finished eating their tuna fish sandwiches and were ripping open the cellophane wrappers of squashed chocolate cupcakes. A mixture of love, joy, and excitement was flowing through her as her heart cherished his proposal. She was being offered the opportunity to spend every night for the rest of her life cradled in Dillon's arms. Visions of last night flashed across her mind; their love-making was far from boring.

With love lighting her eyes she smiled up at Dillon. It was on the tip of her tongue to shout yes when the raised voices of the boys caught her attention.

"You're a jerk!" one of them yelled. Then chaos erupted. All three boys were arguing about the feeding habits of the red-tail hawk.

In that instant Elizabeth realized that when she answered Dillon, she'd be speaking for both herself and Aaron. Kevin, Kyle, and Aaron were great friends, but could they be brothers? Could they live in the same house day after day, year after year? through graduations, college, weddings, and grandchildren? She wasn't certain. "What about the boys?"

Dillon smiled toward the dueling trio and sighed. "I guess we have to keep them."

A smile tilted up the corners of her mouth. "I guess we do." The fight was beginning to die down now, but her tone was serious. "Shouldn't we ask them how they feel?"

"No."

"Oh."

"Listen, Elizabeth. I love you, you love me, and the boys like each other. Everything will work out. When we tell them we're getting married, they'll be thrilled." He gently tilted her face up. Looking into her dark eyes he asked, "Will you marry me?" Dillon watched as the love and happiness in her eyes turned to uncertainty. "Are you worried about Kevin and Kyle?"

"Good Lord, no. Any mother would be proud to call them her sons." She added, a little daunted, "If we get married, that would make me a stepmother."

He placed a kiss on the tip of her nose. "Will you be a wicked stepmother?"

"Only when you want me to."

He suddenly turned serious. "Are you concerned about me becoming Aaron's father?"

A look of incredibility flashed across Elizabeth's face. "That never entered my mind." She took a deep breath. "I'm hesitant for the two of us to make a decision that will affect five people."

"Okay, love, I see your point. Since this is like a family vacation, there's no better opportunity to prove to you that we are the perfect family. By the end of these four days I want an answer."

"Thank you."

"For what?"

"For time and understanding," she whispered, smiling. "I'll show you a proper thank-you for your love, later." With a graceful movement she stood and headed for Dillon's backpack. "I hope you boys saved us something to eat."

Dillon's smile could have lit Times Square. By Friday afternoon Elizabeth would be begging him to marry her. This was going to be the perfect family vacation. What could possibly go wrong?

"Dillon, those clouds don't look so good."

He cast a glance upward. He had to admit the sky was turning a dark, ugly gray. "We might be in for a shower. Let's cook dinner now, and we can play cards in the tent later."

Elizabeth heard the chorus of agreement from three hungry boys and smiled. Some things never changed. With the help of Dillon and the boys she quickly warmed up the chili and opened a large can of ravioli. The simple meal was devoured with a loaf of Italian bread and a container of home-made macaroni salad.

The boys were finishing the dishes when a light drizzle started. They all reached a hurried consensus. They would take their showers and then start a Go Fish tournament.

Five people huddled around the propane lantern that cast a circle of light in the middle of the tent. Grotesque shadows swayed against the darkened sides of the canvas tent, and the steady pounding of rain drummed on. "Give me all of your fours."

Elizabeth flashed a gleeful smile. "Go fish."

With a slight frown Dillon reached for the top card, a nine. How could he be holding eight different cards with no pairs? Elizabeth had a pair of fives and eights showing. Each one of his sons boasted three pairs each, while Aaron, the card shark, had seven pairs lying faceup.

Dillon reached for another chocolate chip cookie and listened to the sound of rain pelt against the roof of the tent. Slowly savoring the cookie, he watched Elizabeth ask Kyle for his threes. She looked cuddly and warm in a pink sweat suit and pair of white socks she had borrowed from him. The yellowish light played across her face, which was bare of any makeup, and reflected off her dark braid that hung over her shoulder. The temperature had dropped twenty degrees since dinner, and the wind had escalated to a small bluster. All the boys were wearing sweat suits and spring jackets, and Kyle had draped his sleeping bag over his shoulders. In a move that took everyone by surprise, Aaron asked Kevin for all his eights, and then went on to win the third straight game.

"Aaron's cheating."

Dillon looked at his youngest son and sighed. The boys were becoming irritable. Two adults and three children confined in an eight-by-eight-foot tent for two hours was asking a lot. "Kyle, Aaron's not cheating," Dillon said. "He's on a winning streak, that's all. Now, please apologize to him."

"No."

Dillon's youngest son looked mutinous. His wild thatch of red hair not only reflected his wicked temper but the stubbornness of a mule. With an apologetic smile to Elizabeth and Aaron he tried to reason with Kyle. "Just because Aaron has won is no reason to call him names. You beat Elizabeth and me, and you don't see us calling you names." Dillon leaned forward and picked up the cards. "I think we're all tired. Let's get some sleep. I'm sure it will clear up by morning and we can go hiking again."

Ignoring Elizabeth's groan, Dillon helped straighten up and tucked the boys in. He followed her out of the tent, and they made a mad dash for his. Inside they were dismayed at what they discovered; a soaking wet sleeping bag, a soggy pillow and a damp duffel bag. The tent Elizabeth had borrowed leaked like a toddler.

Dillon plastered a false smile on his face. "No problem. You sleep in the van and I'll take the back seat of your car."

She moved the sleeping bag out of the small river of water rushing through the tent. "No."

Dillon held the lantern higher. "Why not?"

"Because that would leave the boys outside alone. We wouldn't be able to hear them if a bear attacked or anything else happened to them."

Upon reflection, Dillon had to agree that it would be lousy for the adults to be safe, warm, and dry while the three small boys roughed it. The chances of a bear attack were nonexistent; he'd never heard of bears taking up scuba diving. The only other problem he could foresee was trout spawning in the boys' sleeping bags. But she was right. "Okay, I'll sleep in with the boys. I can afford to be generous and give up one night with you." He tenderly placed a kiss on her lips. "I will have you for the rest of my life."

The rest of Dillon's life seemed in danger of being shortened, permanently. At two o'clock the boys' tent sprang a leak, and he moved them into the van with Elizabeth. He headed for the back seat of her car, taking the last dry comforter. He had peace and quiet to finish out the remainder of the night, and all the food. She was stuck with three excited boys and rain that sounded like machine-gun fire when it hit the roof. Kyle's sleeping bag and pillow were soaked, so the three boys had to share the two remaining dry ones and pack into the back of the van like sardines. But their spirits weren't dampened. They were happy and noisy, while her socks were damp. Elizabeth was miserable—wet and cold. With a muttered oath she pulled her sleeping bag over her head and prayed for sleep or death, she wasn't sure which she would prefer.

At eight the next morning, Dillon climbed into the driver's seat and quietly shut the door. He threw his comforter on the passenger seat, toweled some rain from his hair, and glanced in the back at his sleeping passengers. He guessed Elizabeth was buried under the largest bundle on the back seat. He counted three heads barely visible from under an open sleeping bag on the back floor.

Eight o'clock and the rain hadn't let up. The fog was thick and gave no promise of clearing. Dillon was gong to make the best of whatever happened. He started the van and slowly made his way to the restrooms.

After waking the boys and sending them off to get dressed, he slowly lowered Elisabeth's covers. "Wake up, Sleeping Beauty," he said gently. Her nose wrinkled up slightly, then she sank deeper into the mound of blankets, pulling the edge of the sleeping bag back over her eyes. Dillon tugged at the covers again. "Rise and shine."

Elizabeth sighed. Slowly opening her right eye she saw Dillon wide-awake and grinning. She turned her head to look out the window at the thick fog that could have blanketed London. "Oh, Lord, I'm in a Stephen King nightmare."

"No, you're not. You are alive and well and camping in Virginia."

Still peeking out with one eye, she said, "What can I bribe you with to let me sleep for one more hour?"

"Never offer a starving man a feast when three boys are due back any minute."

"Where are they?"

"Getting dressed. We're parked outside the restrooms." He reached into the front seat and picked up the pile of clothes. "These are yours. Wear my sweat shirt. You didn't pack very warm clothes."

"It's July. I wasn't expecting near blizzard conditions."

"I know. I packed an extra, so wear it." He placed a light kiss on the tip of her nose. "Hurry up and I'll spring for a nice hot breakfast, complete with coffee."

Elizabeth raised her arms and encircled his neck. Pulling his mouth down toward hers, she whispered, "You are a very nice man."

He broke the kiss. "It really is amazing what you'll do for coffee. Remember how nice I am Friday when you answer my question."

Elizabeth was now warm, dressed in Dillon's Penn State sweat shirt, and happily sipping her second cup of coffee. She watched as Kyle and Kevin fought over the last piece of toast. With the skill of a professional referee she picked up a knife and sliced the toast exactly down the middle. She handed each of the boys a piece and continued to listen as Dillon explained about the adjoining bedrooms at the lodge that he'd rented for the next two nights. One room was for the boys and him, the other was for her. "You don't have any objections?"

"To a nice warm, dry bed?"

"I didn't think you would. Since we can't check in until after lunch, how about if we break down camp and hit a Laundromat to dry everything we can?"

Elizabeth smiled at the boys' chorus of "yuks." "Sounds okay with me. Are we going into the town of Luray?"

"We could. Why?"

"I was hoping to see Luray Caverns while we are here. Since it's still raining I figured today would be the perfect day for going underground."

"Gee, Mrs. Lancaster," asked Kyle, "how far underground do we go?"

"I'm not sure, Kyle. I'll let the tour guide fill you in on the details. Now, the sooner you boys help us clean up our campsites the quicker we'll see the stalactites and stalagmites."

"What are they, Mom?"

She smiled at Dillon. "All I'm saying is they're bigger than a bread box."

"Hey, Dad, how big is a bread box?"

Chuckling, Dillon picked up the bill and headed for the cashier. "Sorry, Elizabeth. My boys led a deprived childhood, no bread boxes."

Seven hours later Elizabeth was happy and content as she entered her beige hotel room. Dillon and the boys had the connecting room and were noisily putting their clothes away. Her calf muscles were protesting from the three-mile hike yesterday and the hours spent on her feet today. But at least she could take a hot shower. She reached into her suitcase for the nicest outfit she'd brought —khaki slacks and a red sleeveless sweater. Dillon was taking them all out to eat in the lodge's dining room to celebrate the end of the rain. The next two days were supposed to be beautiful.

Elizabeth had just finished brushing her hair when a knock sounded on the connecting door. "Come in."

The three boys, wearing clean jeans and shirts, entered her room, their damp hair brushed neatly in place. Dillon followed, wearing gray canvas pants with a green-and-gray-striped shirt that brought out the tint of red in his hair. He looked devastating.

"Gee, Mom, I got to watch Mr. McKenzie shave."

She glanced up at Dillon's freshly shaved jaw. Sometimes she envied Aaron. "So I see."

"He nicked himself, and you should have heard the words he said."

"Aaron, I believe I apologized for that already. Let's not bore your mother with men stuff." He didn't meet Elizabeth's eyes. "I thought you boys were hungry. Let's go before all the food is gone."

Elizabeth hid a smile at the obvious change of topic and followed the boys from her room.

The dining room held a warm and casual interior, and the food was excellent. Conversation at their table had been nonstop and everyone enjoyed the evening, except Kyle who was unusually quiet and fidgety. When questioned he assured his father nothing was wrong.

It was after ten when Dillon and Elizabeth tucked the boys in. "Hey, Dad, aren't you coming to bed?" asked Kyle.

"Sure, son, after I watch television for a while."

"You can watch it in here."

Dillon smiled at his youngest and said, "No way, boys. I know your plan. If I stay in here to watch TV, you boys would stay up all night with me." With laughter shining in his eyes he turned to Elizabeth. "Can I watch television in your room?"

She was tempted to refuse, just to see the look

on his face. "Okay, but you can't stay too long. I'm beat."

He saw the teasing light in her laughing eyes and decided two can play that game. "I won't stay that long. I need my rest too. Tomorrow we're going on a five-mile hike to see some waterfalls." He heard her groan and smiled. "I'll leave the door open so I can hear you guys."

He looked at Aaron and Kyle in one large bed and asked, "Okay?" At their nods he glanced at Kevin in the other double bed and saw his nod. "Don't hog all the covers before I come back. And you better not snore." At the sound of the boys' giggles, he and Elizabeth wished them a good-night, turned out the lights, and went into her room.

In comfortable silence they watched the end of a police show with the sound turned down so that the screeching tires and flying bullets wouldn't waken the boys. A beer commercial was playing when Dillon took her hand and whispered, "It's only Wednesday night. I don't think I can wait till Friday for your answer."

"I—"

"No, don't say a word. I promised you time." Dillon took a deep breath and continued, "I'm setting a limit. I want my answer at ten A.M. I figure by then you should have had at least two cups of coffee and be somewhat reasonable."

"I'm perfectly reasonable."

Moving slowly toward her, Dillon placed a gentle kiss on the end of her nose. "Not without your coffee fix."

Elizabeth frowned and narrowed her eyes, trying to look mad. Her grandfather had once threat-ened to put the coffeepot in her room so he wouldn't have to face her first thing in the morn-ing. So what? She wasn't a morning person. She wasn't the type of person who waited with bated breath for Mr. Sunshine to make his appearance every morning. If she owned a gun she would personally extinguish the singing of one blue jay who frequented her bedroom window.

Dillon deserved to wake up next to her every morning for the rest of his life for so blatantly stating her one flaw. "How about if I answer your question right now?" she asked.

He noticed the frown pulling down the corners of her mouth and quickly changed tactics. He kissed her. He leisurely lifted his mouth from her moist, responsive one. "I want an answer at ten o'clock Friday, not one moment sooner." With a devilish smile he slowly straightened to give her breathing room. "Do you think the boys are asleep yet?"

She drew in a deep breath and smiled. "I hope so, Mr. McKenzie, because it would probably affect your sons' emotional growth adversely to see their father being locked in a hotel room by a desperate woman."

"Desperate, huh?"

A soft, womanly purr reached his ears—"Only for you"—at the same time that Kyle called his name. She saw the look of indecision in his eyes. "Go see what Kyle wants. I'll be right here."

Ten minutes later she was still waiting and wondering. When she finally couldn't stand the suspense any longer, she headed for the boys' room and located Kyle and Dillon in the bathroom. Kyle's arm and chest were covered in a bright red rash. "Poison ivy?"

Dillon gave her a lopsided grin that spoke of regrets and responsibilities. "Yes. Could you stay with him while I run down to the main desk to see if they have anything we could put on him?"

Distress filled Kyle's eyes.

"How about if I run downstairs and you stay with him?" she suggested. The no was barely out of Dillon's mouth when she cut in. "I'll go. You stay here. He needs his father." Knowing that she was right, she quickly grabbed her purse and headed for the main desk.

She lay awake in a lonely queen-size bed half an hour later and shook her head at the bad luck Dillon and she had run into. First it was the rain, and now poison ivy. It wasn't Dillon's fault, even though he seemed determined to take the blame for both. Elizabeth's love for him grew when Kyle had tearfully asked him not to leave and Dillon quickly replied that he wouldn't have dreamed of it. With an apologetic smile toward Elizabeth he walked her to the door, placed a chaste kiss on her forehead, then closed the door between them.

"Are you sure it's okay for Kyle to go hiking?"

"Elizabeth, he only has poison ivy, not a broken arm."

She glanced at Kyle and admitted he seemed perfectly willing to go into the wilderness dressed in jeans and a T-shirt. Dried pink calamine lotion was caked on his arms and neck, and a smile was spread across his face. "Well, you are his father."

Dillon tenderly cupped her cheek. "Yes, I am his father and he is fine. Tonight I'm sure all the boys will be dead tired from this hike."

Elizabeth read the hidden message in the shining green eyes. "As long as they're the only ones dead tired."

He placed a swift kiss on her parted lips. "I'll think of something to revive you."

"Oh, yuk. They're kissing again," groaned Kyle.

A fiery blush crept up Elizabeth's neck and face as she glanced over at Aaron. She met his smile with one of her own and turned back toward Dillon. "Lead on, Daniel Boone, and show us cute and cuddly forest critters."

A half hour later she had to agree with the boys—this was great. They had spotted two chipmunks, a squirrel, rabbits, two female deer, and one baby doe still marked with his white dots. Dillon had identified two kinds of owls hooting in the dense forest and pointed out what appeared to be bear tracks.

The trail they were following ran parallel to a large creek that boasted numerous waterfalls and some interesting fishing holes, which Dillon claimed were full of trout. Bypassing some tired hikers coming from the opposite direction, Elizabeth realized they had been heading downhill the entire time. The return trip to the van was all uphill . . . and not an elevator in sight. "Dillon dearest, do you realize we have to climb this mountain to get back?"

He picked up on the forced sweetness of her voice and grimaced. "It's only a little hill. Right, boys?"

"Yes, sir."

She shot Dillon a glare that clearly expressed her displeasure at being outnumbered and marched past them, continuing down the path into parts unknown. She was going to hike this trail like a pro. Not one word of complaint would escape her lips. By the time she was done with Shenandoah National Park, they would be begging her to give survival tactics to their rangers.

Dillon watched as Elizabeth raised her chin and flounced past him. She was adorable when mad. Then again, she was adorable when she wasn't. She was just plain adorable, and he was in love. Granted, this vacation wasn't going as smoothly as he had wanted, but nothing had gone wrong so far today, and tonight he'd make sure everything went right. By Friday he'd be a happily engaged man. He smiled with the boys as they headed after Elizabeth and his happiness.

She was thirty feet in front of them when she tumbled to the ground. With the speed of a man possessed he reached her side just as a barely audible curse escaped her lips. "Are you okay?" he asked horrified.

Elizabeth raised herself to a sitting position and started brushing off half the trail dust that clung to her blouse and jeans. "Sure, just bruised my dignity."

He gently cupped her chin and placed a kiss on the end of her dust-covered nose. "I'll kiss your dignity later." He grabbed her hands and pulled her up. She winced as her foot took her weight. "Sit back down and let me look at that foot."

Tears sprang to her eyes as she took a step toward a fallen log nearby. Her left foot wouldn't hold her weight. A startled gasp escaped her throat as Dillon swiftly bent forward, picked her up, and carried her to the log. She watched as Dillon cuffed up her jeans and pulled off her left sneaker and sock.

A frown marred Dillon's brow as he examined the rapidly swelling ankle. "I think it's sprained."

She bit her lower lip to stop its trembling. The only sound to escape her tear-encased throat was a husky "oh."

"Do you know what that means?"

"You're going to shoot me and put me out of my misery."

"No. It means I get to carry you out of here."

Elizabeth looked around at the three wide-eyed boys and mustered a smile. "Think I'll break his back?"

"Wow, Dad. Are you gonna carry her all the way back to the van?"

Dillon raised one finger and gently wiped a single tear that had escaped the reservoir in her brown eyes. "It's either that or leave her here for bear bait." He saw Aaron go pale and quickly reached for the boy and hugged him. "I was only kidding, Aaron. I wouldn't leave your mother here."

His heart filled with love as Aaron returned his hug and whispered, "Thank you."

It was dark by the time they reached their hotel rooms. A doctor in Front Royal proclaimed that Elizabeth's foot was indeed sprained but not seriously. After a heated argument with Dillon she convinced the doctor she was perfectly fine to drive home the following day as long as she stayed off the foot till then. The doctor expertly wrapped the foot and gave Elizabeth a small packet of pain-killers. He instructed her to apply ice packs and keep it elevated. A smiling Elizabeth was carried up to her room by a scowling Dillon, faithfully followed by three boys.

She had won an argument against Dillon concerning dinner. They had stopped at a family restaurant, and with Dillon's help she'd managed to hobble to the nearest table. Over a lingering cup of coffee Dillon had insisted she take a pain pill. She refused. She had explained that medication affected her more strongly than other people and promised to take the pills before her shower.

Dillon left the door open between their rooms as he helped the boys get ready for bed. Elizabeth was attempting to take a shower unassisted, and he wanted to be able to hear her if she called out. Kyle had finished his shower, and Aaron was already in the bathroom when Elizabeth hobbled out of her bathroom. A tender smile erased some of the tension on his face as he noticed her pajamas.

She wore a long white T-shirt with Garfield— decorated like a Christmas tree—printed on the front. She had attempted to unbraid her long hair and work a brush through it. In her left hand she trailed the Ace bandage from her foot. Her eyes held a glassy, spaced-out look.

"Did you take the pain-killers?"

Her voice was slurred. "Two, right before I took the shower."

A look of amusement crossed Dillon's face as he rushed across the room and helped her into the bed. He lovingly placed a pillow under the injured ankle and instructed Kevin to run to the ice machine at the end of the hall and fill the ice bag he had purchased in Front Royal. By the time Kevin returned, Elizabeth was sound asleep. She never felt Dillon gently place the bag over her swollen ankle.

Nine-thirty the next morning Elizabeth was awakened by the aroma of freshly perked coffee. She opened her eyes slowly and saw Dillon place a tray with coffee and a danish on the small table directly in front of the window. The curtains were drawn back, and a gorgeous day sparkled on the other side of the glass. The lodge was built on the top of a mountain, and they had a breathtaking view of stately mountains, rolling hills, and endless trees—all of it green, as far as her eyes could see, light green, dark green, and the green of Dillon's eyes. With a shy smile and a yawn, she said, "Good morning."

"It's almost afternoon."

"What time is it?"

Nervously Dillon ran his hand through his hair. "You still have half an hour."

She didn't need an explanation; it was almost ten. She took the cup he handed her. "Where are the boys?"

"There's a stable here and they advertised hay rides and the boys wanted to go, so I bought them tickets. They should be back by eleven."

Elizabeth drank the last of the coffee. "Are you expecting trouble?"

Dillon stopped pacing in front of the window and glared at her. "Of course I'm expecting trouble. What kind of woman would want to marry me after this fiasco. Our tents were collapsed by a monsoon, the boys haven't stopped bickering once, you practically caught pneumonia sleeping in the van, Kyle breaks out in poison ivy and expects my undivided attention, and now you can't even walk."

She hid a secret smile behind her cup. "You forgot one thing."

He wondered which catastrophe he'd overlooked. "What?"

"I love you."

Happiness shone in his eyes as he slowly removed the empty cup from her hand and sat on the edge of the mattress. With a trembling finger he gently traced her sensual lower lip. "Answer my question."

"Is it ten yet?"

"No, but who the hell cares?"

"You're such a romantic. Ask me just like you did while we were sitting in heaven."

"Elizabeth Sarah Lancaster, would you do me the honor of becoming my wife?"

She reached up and wrapped her arms around his neck and slowly brought his mouth down. When his lips were barely a breath away a soft yes was whispered against them.

Elizabeth felt the demand of Dillon's lips and answered with a soft purr. His kiss tasted of coffee and promises. With a boldness born of love, she broke the kiss and whispered, "Make love to me."

"Gladly," was muffled harshly against the delicate arch of her throat. In one swift movement he pulled her nightshirt over her head and gently cupped her breasts. The feel of her dainty fingers unbuckling his belt sent a shaft of burning desire straight to his aroused manhood. With hasty movements he pulled off his shirt and finished kicking off his jeans before lying down next to her.

Hunger blazed in his eyes as he stared at the only piece of clothing between them—a silken pair of yellow panties with a monarch butterfly embroidered on them. With great deliberation he slowly bent forward and placed a heated kiss on the orange-and-black decoration. "How's your foot?"

"What foot?"

He chuckled. "I think I'm going to start a butterfly collection."

Eleven

Elizabeth glanced at Aaron sitting in the passenger seat and asked, "Do you like Mr. McKenzie?"

"Sure, Mom. He lets me keep Bubba in his bathroom."

A quick glance in the rearview mirror showed Dillon's van directly behind her. She had just learned of Bubba's existence. "I guess I'll finally get to meet the famous Bubba when we get home?"

"Can he come live at our house?"

"We'll see. Do you like Kyle and Kevin?"

"Yeah."

Somewhere there must be a book on how to tell your kids you're getting married, but right now she had no time to find it. Dillon had insisted they tell their sons on the way home. She was to stop at the rest area in West Virginia, meet Dillon, and compare notes on the boys' reactions. "If you could have brothers, would you pick Kevin and Kyle?"

"I guess so."

Elizabeth glanced at the sign she'd just passed and groaned. Two miles to the rest area. "How would you feel about me marrying Mr. McKenzie?"

"Is that why you're always kissing him?"

Determined not to blush she answered, "Sort of."

"Would he be my dad?"

"He'll be your stepfather. It would be up to you if you want to call him dad."

Aaron's voice was low when he asked, "Do you think he'll let me call him dad?"

Elizabeth wiped at her eyes as she pulled off onto the exit ramp and parked the car in front of the restrooms. She unfastened his seat belt and hugged him. Her voice cracked when she answered, "I think he'd like that very much."

In a flurry of motion three doors of Dillon's van flew open. Kevin and Kyle yanked open Aaron's door and practically dragged him from the car. Amidst all the shouting and confusion she heard Kyle shout, "Neat," and Kevin spout, "Radical." A smile lit her face as she watched the boys punch each other and race for the soda machine. It wasn't going to be as easy as the boys thought, but they did have a great beginning.

"Elizabeth, we've been back from Virginia for almost a week and we still haven't set the date."

She glanced up from the cake she was decorating and smiled. "Impatient?"

"Hell, yes." Her smile widened as he added, "And frustrated. Since we have been home I've been working fourteen-hour days to catch up on my work, and you have been busy trying to put Betty Crocker out of business." There was a note of desperation in his voice. "I need a kiss."

"Well, why didn't you say so?" Placing her baker's tube filled with blue frosting on the table, she rushed into his arms and kissed him like a movie siren.

Dillon felt the hunger in her kiss and groaned in frustration. The boys were twenty feet away, in her living room watching a movie. He used every ounce of willpower to break the kiss. "We need to talk."

Elizabeth lightly ran her hands down his shirt and marveled at the strength concealed beneath it. He wanted to talk, and she wanted to lock him in her bedroom for the next year or so. Maybe by then she wouldn't mind the constant intrusions of the world.

He sighed at the dreamy expression in her eyes. She really played unfair sometimes. "How much baking do you have left to do tonight?"

"Only a couple of hours' worth. Why?"

"It's the boys' bedtime so I have to be going. How would you like to meet me out by the old rose arbor, around eleven, for a picnic?"

"A picnic?"

Dillon smiled mysteriously. "Meet me there at eleven." His smile was still in place as he called his sons and headed home.

Elizabeth squinted into the darkness. She could barely make out his shape reclining on a blanket. "Dillon?"

"Who else were you expecting?"

She kicked off her sandals as she sat down. "No lights?"

"Don't need them, and besides it might attract attention." With a gentle tug he eased her into a reclining position beside him. "This is ideal. From here you can see your back screen door and hear if Aaron calls you and I can keep an eye on my sons."

She snuggled closer to him. "Mmmmm." She closed her eyes and breathed the cool evening air. She wondered why it felt so wonderful lying in an old Victorian rose garden. A partially rotted, dilapidated frame was all that remained of what once was an exquisite rose arbor. There were red clay bricks scattered between patches of dirt and grass and a few of the heartier varieties of roses still managed to bloom in between the weeds. The most fascinating feature of the garden was an old, tarnished, bronze sundial.

Tonight, without any light from the moon, it was impossible to distinguish the rose arbor, let alone the sundial or brick paths. Elizabeth knew every nook and cranny of the garden. Living next door and loving to work in her yard, she had always felt sad about the neglected garden. "Are you going to rebuild the garden?"

He rested her head on his shoulder. "No, we are. It will be your garden, too, or have you forgotten?"

"How could I have forgotten? You remind me, at least once every day." Nestled comfortably in Dillon's embrace, she studied the stars above. "What kind of wedding do you want?"

"Fast."

"Dillon!"

"Okay, you name different kinds of weddings and I'll tell you what I think."

"Justice of the peace."

"Too impersonal."

"Eloping to Las Vegas."

"Too callous."

"How about a church ceremony?"

"A big, elaborate affair? or small and intimate?" Her voice was soft and dreamy. "Small and intimate."

Dillon tightened his hold and placed a soft kiss on her temple. "Is that what you want?"

"There's one other kind of wedding." She hesitated before she said, "A garden ceremony."

He knew what was coming. "As in a rose garden, complete with arbor and fancy brick walks?"

Elizabeth heard the acceptance in his voice and quickly turned to face him. "You'd marry me right here, in this garden?"

He groaned. "If you would have said a moon wedding, I would have called NASA in the morning to find out when the next space shuttle was scheduled."

"I love you, Dillon James McKenzie."

Tenderly brushing back a stray wisp of her hair, he settled her back into the crook of his shoulder. "I love you, too, but no more kissing. We are here to talk and we can't do that if our mouths are occupied kissing each other senseless. Now that we know where we are getting married, we need to set a date."

She closed her eyes and tried to visualize what the garden would look like in its formal splendor. The arbor would be glistening white with hundreds of roses climbing its trellis, and brilliant, spring sunshine would reflect off the shimmering sundial. Butterflies would be fluttering around newly planted flowers. The preacher would be standing in the arbor with Dillon, who would be dressed all in white. She'd march down the aisle made of brick wearing a pale yellow dress to match the morning light, and all three boys would be dashing in their light gray suits. "May or June would be perfect."

Dillon's mind went into shock. "Of next year?"

"We missed this year," she said, laughing.

"No, no, no. You seem to have missed the point, Elizabeth. I said I wanted a fast wedding. I was thinking about August."

"That's next month!"

"I know. I thought it would be better to get married before the boys start back to school."

She mentally said good-bye to a garden wedding. "You're right. As soon as the kids go back to school they're busy with friends and teachers, and then comes Halloween followed by Thanksgiving and Christmas."

Dillon picked up on the note of despair in her voice. "I promised you a garden wedding. I'll call some local landscapers tomorrow and see what they can do."

"That's going to be expensive."

He tenderly brushed a kiss across her cheek. "Mmmmm, consider it your wedding present."

"A whole garden?"

"Yes, but you're the one who has to work with the landscapers. I wouldn't know a petunia from a pansy."

In a flash Elizabeth rolled over onto his chest and proceeded to kiss him senseless. Her hands threaded in his hair as he opened his mouth to her demanding one. Heat ignited and passion soared.

Feeling her light weight move in a rhythm as old as Eve was creating a strain on his control. With determination he broke the fierce kiss. "I haven't offered you anything to eat."

Elizabeth peered into the darkness surrounding them. "You really brought food?"

After lovingly assisting her to a sitting position he reached behind him and produced a bucket filled with ice cubes and soda cans. With a great flourish he pulled out a freezing-cold can, popped the top, and handed it to her. Setting his can beside his leg, he put the bucket back and brought forth a bag of pretzels.

Elizabeth thanked him and reached in to sample a few. As she chewed on the salty snack, she wondered what else Dillon had planned now that the wedding was settled. She had felt his response to her kiss, and knew whatever else he wanted to discuss must be important. Deciding the best course of action was none, she waited in the darkness for him to speak. She didn't have to wait long.

"Do you mind living in my house?"

Was he really worried about that? Did he think she'd mind moving from a small two-bedroom cottage into a five-bedroom, two-and-a-half-baths house complete with family room and dining room? "No, I don't mind. Should I?"

"I wasn't sure. You seem to like the house. But liking a house and living in it are two different things."

"Oh, I guess we never discussed houses before."

"There's a lot we haven't discussed before. That's why we are going to sit here and talk. No more kissing." He was quiet a moment. "Name one thing you'll change about the house."

"Bubba would have to move out of the bathroom."

"Done. Did Aaron show you Bubba's latest trick?"

"Besides riding the skateboard through the hall?"

"Hey, I taught him that, and he loves it." Reaching for his soda, he said, "Aaron found a miniature ball and Bubba pushes it around the bathroom. It looks like he's trying to play soccer. Kyle and Aaron are going out tomorrow looking for more turtles. They want to start a team."

"Oh, good Lord. You have to stop them."

"Me?"

"Okay, we. One turtle in the house is plenty." She decided it was her turn to ask a question. "Don't you think I should meet your parents and family before the wedding?"

"Normally I would say yes, but since Dad and Mom retired to Idaho last year, it's senseless for them to come out here twice. They'll be here for the wedding." Sensing her need for reassurance, he said, "Don't worry, they're going to love you and Aaron."

Elizabeth thought over his answer and decided he knew his parents better than anyone else. If he wasn't concerned about their reaction, neither was she. "Do you know something else we haven't thought about?"

Dillon could name a very important aspect of their lives they hadn't discussed: her career. How were they to function as a normal family when she spent night after night baking into the wee hours of the morning? She barely had time now. What would happen when she became a wife and a mother of two more? Silently praying she'd bring up her business and secretly dreading it, he asked, "What?"

"Rufus tries to eat Snapdragon. How are they going to live in the same house?"

"They will adjust. If I had to place money on those two, I'd back Snapdragon."

Dillon looked around the pitch dark garden and heard Elizabeth yawn. It was past midnight and the morning always seemed to come too quickly. They might not have discussed any important topics besides the wedding, but it was a beginning. Next time he would bring up children. He could live with Elizabeth's wishes on that matter. If she wanted more, great. If she thought three were enough, he could live with that. But a little girl would be nice . . .

The one subject that plagued his dreams was Indescribably Delicious. He still felt guilty about Rachael and the sacrifices she'd made. He'd been given a second chance, and this time he wouldn't blow it. Elizabeth obviously loved her business, and he was going to do everything within his power to make sure it was a success.

Dillon rose to his feet and pulled Elizabeth to hers. "Come on, sleepy head. I'll walk you home."

• • •

"Elizabeth, could you come over? I've got Dan Cramer from Countryside Landscaping here."

"Sure. Give me ten minutes and I'll be there." As Elizabeth hung up the phone she marveled at Dillon's determination. He'd certainly hired the grounds people quickly.

When she got outside, Dillon was in his backyard showing the landscaper the scope of the job. He saw Elizabeth hurry around the side of his house and smiled. "Dan, I would like to introduce you to Elizabeth Lancaster, my fiancée."

"Ms. Lancaster."

"Call me Elizabeth."

Dillon placed his arm around her shoulder. "I've already told Dan you have carte blanche on the entire yard. I have to get back to work now, but you explain to Dan what you want done so he can work up a preliminary estimate." After gently kissing her cheek he headed back to the house.

As he reached the door, Dillon called out one last instruction. "One thing, Dan. The entire project has to be completed by the last weekend in August. We're getting married in the garden."

A look of horror passed across Dan's weathered features as he looked around the neglected yard. "He's kidding?"

"Afraid not."

"We're not looking at a couple of trees and some yews are we?"

"Afraid not." She smiled, looking at the deteriorated arbor. "I want it brought back to its former glory, complete with rose arbor, sundial, and brick walks. I realize you can't pull a Victorian garden from midair, but I'll settle for the foundation."

Blood ran back into Dan's pale cheeks as he visualized the garden. Here was a woman who wasn't afraid to be different. In today's world everyone wanted things quick and easy with no maintenance. He was tired of planting yews and dogwoods surrounded by tons of mulch. Here was a challenge, an actual garden to be completed within five weeks.

Two hours later, Elizabeth shook Dan's hand and promised to be home the following night when he came by with the estimate for Dillon. She walked into her future home and noticed Dillon's office door was closed. She gathered up the boys, left a note, and headed for the pool.

As she slid a tray of cupcakes into her oven she felt arms slide around her waist and smiled. After closing the oven door she leaned back into his embrace and tilted her face up for a hello kiss.

"You smell good."

"It's orange extract."

"It's sexy as hell."

"I'll call up a cosmetic company and make a fortune." She turned into his embrace and reached up for a second, more satisfying kiss.

Dillon broke the kiss and nipped tenderly at her exposed ear lobe. "Where are the boys?"

Regret tinged her voice. "Playing in Aaron's room."

"Do you think Aaron would like to sleep over?"

"I'm sure he would, but I can't come."

"Why not?"

"Betsy Lou's birthday party is tomorrow."

He ran heated lips down her arched throat and asked, "What's that got to do with us?"

"I need three dozen cupcakes decorated with ballerina slippers, an orange layer cake, and two sheet cakes by ten o'clock in the morning. Friday nights are my busiest."

Dillon kept his face hidden as he placed kisses across her collar bone. Inward a battle raged. One part of him wanted to scream, *The hell with Betsy Lou. What about us?* The more sensible side reasoned, *This is her job, her choice of professions.* She never disturbed him while he was working. For that matter she usually took the boys swimming or to her house so he could concentrate.

He was supposed to be giving her fatherhood lessons in payment for that peace and quiet. Guilt descended on his shoulders. So far she had kept up her end of the bargain, while his end had slipped away. "How about I take Aaron anyway? It would give you some time."

Elizabeth looked up at Dillon and wondered, *Time for what?* She was planning to spend the remainder of the night in the kitchen baking. "Sure, if you're sure it's no problem."

He lightly ran his thumb over her lower lip. "In five weeks, he'll be living there, so he might as well get used to it. I'll go get the boys." A frown pulled at the corners of Elizabeth's lips as she watched Dillon and the boys head home.

By one o'clock Dillon called it a night and headed for bed. He had allowed the boys to stay up till ten to watch a movie. After safely tucking Aaron in Kyle's room, he spent fifteen minutes gathering up dirty laundry. He had washed three loads of clothes, scrubbed the kitchen floor, and straightened up the family room.

With a new perspective he slowly walked through every room of his house and sighed. It was too big. He and the boys barely kept it liveable, much less clean. The living room and dining room were virtually empty; he hadn't gotten around to buying furniture yet. Two bedrooms upstairs were empty, and the attic contained Christmas decorations and cobwebs. Dust covered every stick of furniture, and the bathrooms needed a good cleaning. There just weren't enough hours in the day.

How was Elizabeth going to manage? With a grimace he visualized her sparkling clean house: her windows glistened, you could eat off her kitchen floor, and the throw pillows on her couch were always fluffed.

Dillon considered himself a modern man, especially since Rachael had passed away. He'd made sure the boys had three meals a day. They might not be square meals, more like oblong, but they were healthy. He always tried to do the laundry before someone ran out of something. Dirty dishes were usually packed in the dishwasher. And if dust got a little thick, no one complained.

Marriage to Elizabeth was going to be a partnership. They'd share the good with the bad. And if that meant the housework, he'd pull his weight. He looked out his bedroom window and saw her kitchen lights still blaring, and frowned. He climbed into his lonely bed and mentally made a list of things to do. First was to clean the bathrooms and get the boys to dust. He had about five hours' worth of work to do in his office and then he'd take Elizabeth and Aaron out for their usual Saturday night pizza. Sunday morning he'd make sure his boys attended Sunday school, and then he'd build Bubba a box. Somehow he'd make enough hours in the day. He closed his eyes and dreamed of Elizabeth sharing his bed.

It was after one when Elizabeth shut off the lights in the kitchen and stared out into the darkness. Everyone must be asleep at Dillon's house. Not one light was shining. Loneliness settled in her heart. She wanted to be over there snuggled deep in Dillon's embrace, with her family safely sleeping around her. The love she felt for Dillon was immeasurable, and his sons had wormed their way into her heart. A soft smile curved her lips as she thought about Aaron. He had changed so much in the past couple of months. He had grown from a quiet, shy boy to a talkative, active youngster. A small chuckle vibrated in her throat as she pictured the scene she had walked into the other day. She had entered Dillon's house unannounced and caught the boys sliding down the banister with Aaron gleefully in the middle.

Soon they'd be a complete family. All she had to do was wait. With a weary shrug of her shoulders she headed for a hot shower and a soft bed.

Six days later Dillon stood by the French doors of his office and glared into his backyard. Elizabeth was standing in the middle of mass confusion and laughing at something Dan Cramer had said. She was wearing a pair of khaki shorts that showed off her tanned legs, and a purple blouse. Ever since six o'clock Monday morning when the landscapers had shown up, he hadn't had a moment's privacy with her.

Every morning she greeted the crew and discussed their days' activities with Dan. By ten she always left on delivers and any errands she had to do, usually taking all three boys with her. Then came lunch, swimming, and more discussions with Dan. Dinner followed, along with hours of baking, which were topped off with solitary, exhausted sleep.

Meanwhile, he tried to work, without too much success, while backhoes, carpenters, and muscle-bound college students without shirts tore up his backyard.

Being an architect had some advantages, like designing turtle houses. With Aaron's help he had built Bubba an estate. The huge box sitting on the porch contained a bedroom, kitchen, swimming pool, and soccer field. Elizabeth had been duly impressed. She patted Bubba's bald head and dashed off to the printers to order wedding invitations.

Frustration built as he watched Elizabeth run over to an old pickup truck and smile brilliantly. For the first time since Dan's crew had begun, Dillon left his office and headed for his future wife.

By the time he walked outside, Elizabeth had climbed into the back of the truck. A smile softened his features as he watched her lovingly trace the Roman numerals engraved on the bronze sundial Dan had found.

She knew the minute Dillon stepped up to the truck. Tears filled her eyes as she traced the numeral eleven. In exactly twenty-eight days, when the shadow of the dial fell on this eleven, she would become Mrs. Dillon McKenzie. Suddenly she climbed out of the truck and ran straight into Dillon's arms. She caught his surprised mouth in a heated kiss, totally unaware of the whistles and catcalls from the crew.

As he carried her toward the house, Dillon called over his shoulder, "Dan, find another one of those sundials."

Glancing across the table, Dillon noticed the dark shadows under Elizabeth's eyes. "Tired?"

"Yes, but in three and a half weeks it will all be over."

He silently wondered if she was going to make it. Every day the shadows became more pronounced, and yesterday he had heard her actually snap at Aaron. Tonight he had invited Aaron and her to dinner. He had cooked spaghetti and picked up a loaf of Italian bread in an attempt to lighten her load and show her he didn't mind cooking. He had even picked up a cherry pie so that she could enjoy a dessert she hadn't slaved over.

Taking a sip of her coffee she glanced at the boxed pie and grimaced. She was marrying a man who bought pies off the grocery shelf. Didn't he like her pies? "Don't forget tomorrow night you and the boys have an appointment to be measured for your tuxes."

"I won't." He refilled his cup. "Is there something I could do to help?"

"No, everything is under control. The invitations are out, the garden's coming along nicely, and the caterers have been booked."

"What about renting some chairs?"

"Done."

"Preacher?"

"Taken care of."

"I wish there was something I could do for you."

It was on the tip of her tongue to ask him to go over to her house and clean the oven; it was a mess. Instead she asked, "Could you watch Aaron tomorrow afternoon?"

"Sure, where are you going?"

"Shopping for a dress." She got up from the table and automatically finished loading the dishwasher.

"Stop that."

"What?"

"I can take care of the dishes. I don't expect you to do something I'm capable of."

Elizabeth looked at the stubborn set of his jaw and sat down to finish her coffee.

"I'm sorry, I didn't mean to snap at you."

"That's okay, Dillon. I understand." She didn't understand at all. Why didn't he want her to load a dishwasher for heaven's sake. He spent his time cooking the meal; the least she could do was help clean up.

Dillon read the confusion and hurt in her eyes and groaned. He gently pulled her to her feet and led her into his office. "I want to show you something."

Elizabeth watched as he locked the door and closed the drapes against the approaching darkness. "What did you want to show me?"

He pulled her into his aching arms and tenderly kissed her willing mouth. "How much I love you."

Half an hour later Elizabeth lay on the braided rug cradled in his arms. She felt totally and properly loved. "Are you sure the boys are okay?"

"If they aren't, they would have yelled." He ran his hand down her heated back and felt desire rekindle. "You better put your clothes on. I can't guarantee we wouldn't be interrupted the second time."

Her chuckle filled the room as she sat up and reached for her clothes. She was braiding her hair when Dillon spoke. "What do you think of children?"

"At this moment I love children. If one would have knocked on that door twenty minutes ago, my answer wouldn't be the same."

Dillon slipped his foot into his sneaker. "Did you ever think about having any more?"

She caught the seriousness of his question and studied his closed expression. For the first time she couldn't read him. She wasn't sure if he wanted more or not. She told him the truth. "A little girl would be nice."

"Big brown eyes and dark hair?"

She saw the sparkle in his eyes and laughingly sat on his lap. "No, red hair and mischievous green eyes." Cradled in his secure arms she closed her eyes and dreamed of their future.

She'd be the best mother and wife since Donna Reed. She'd keep the kids quiet while Dillon worked. When the kids came in from playing in the snow, hot chocolate would be warming on the stove and cookies would be baking in the oven.

For the first time in seven years she'd be a full-time mother and wife. She wouldn't have to worry about baking other people's cakes and cookies. She'd have a husband, three boys, and a huge house to take care of. And maybe one day, God willing, a daughter with her father's smile.

Twelve

Dillon glanced at the mound of laundry piled in the hallway and grimaced. He'd spent the past two hours cleaning the boys' rooms. No wonder Kevin and Kyle never seemed to have anything to wear. Dirty clothes were hidden under beds, thrown into closets, and shoved into toy boxes—everywhere but where they belonged: in the hamper. He picked up a bag of garbage and an armful of laundry and headed downstairs for the vacuum. The bedrooms were in pretty decent shape or would be, as soon as the boys finished dusting and picking up while he ran the vacuum.

How do mothers cope with the never-ending chores? For the past two weeks he'd spent hours scrubbing floors, polishing woodwork, and scouring toilets. He had tied a T-shirt to the end of a broom and knocked down cobwebs, combatted ring around the collar, and actually roasted a chicken. With an exhausted sigh he realized everything needed to be done again. It was a vicious cycle of thankless chores. No one ever said, "Thanks, Dad, for the clean socks," or "Gee, Dad, the bathtub sure shines." The only thing he heard was,

"Dad, where's my bathing suit," or "Dad, where did you put my skateboard?"

He went down the cellar steps and dumped the armful of laundry into the already overflowing basket and sighed. What kind of woman would want to face this day after day? No wonder Rachael was dissatisfied, and they had only lived in a two-bedroom condominium. Dillon opened the lid to the washer, packed it with the boys' sheets, and added detergent. He placed an affectionate pat on his brand new dryer and headed back upstairs, deciding a laundry chute was definitely needed.

Fifteen minutes later he hauled his tool box up to Kyle's room and ripped apart the vacuum. With a scowl he pulled a disfigured green plastic army man from the roller. "Kyle, I thought I told you to pick up this room."

"Sorry, Dad."

"Yeah. Go make sure Kevin is picking up his room. You two have to learn to take care of your stuff. I don't have all day to pick up after you."

As he left the room, Kyle muttered, "Gee, Dad, why don't we get a maid?"

Dillon was refastening the guard on the vacuum when his son's sarcastic reply hit him: a maid. Why hadn't he thought of that? No, not a maid but a cleaning lady, some nice woman to help out around the house for a couple of hours a day. Elizabeth would have enough to worry about with her new family and her business. She wouldn't have time to think about wax buildup and streaked windows.

A rich laugh boomed from Kyle's room. That problem was easily solved, and by a seven-year-old kid, no less.

In the next room Kevin and Kyle, hearing their father laugh out loud, shrugged their shoulders. With a shake of his head, Kevin muttered, "He's sure acting strange since Mrs. Lancaster said she'd marry him."

Elizabeth hung up the phone and smiled. She'd just turned down an order for a sheet cake. With a thick red crayon she marked off another day on her wall calendar. Nine days left until she became Mrs. Dillon McKenzie.

A dreamy smile curved her lips as she thought about Dillon. She missed him. She hadn't seen him since dinner the previous night. He had had to go home and work, and she had had three pies and a batch of oatmeal cookies to bake. "Aaron?"

Her son came walking into the kitchen. "Yes, Mom."

"I'm going over to see Dillon for a minute. Want to come and see Kyle?"

"Sure."

She quietly let herself into his office and noticed the curtains were drawn closed. Was it to keep out the sunlight or the sight and sounds of workmen? With extreme care she turned the lock and tiptoed over to where Dillon sat at his drafting table with his back to her.

He smelled apple pie and cinnamon bread the moment before her dainty hands covered his eyes. "Guess who?"

"The Pillsbury Dough Boy?"

Elizabeth shook his head no. He tried again.

"Amelia Earhart?"

"One more try and if it isn't right, I'm leaving," was whispered hoarsely against his ear.

In a sudden movement he swung around and lifted her onto his lap. "I was thinking about you."

She forced her lips into a pout. "No, you weren't. You were working. You haven't thought about me since I fed you dinner last night."

Fire burned in his eyes as he leaned down and tenderly sucked her lower lip between his teeth and gently bit it. At the feel of arms sliding around his neck he released her lip and trailed kisses down her throat. "I thought about you while I worked last night. I thought about you in the shower. Mostly I thought about you in my bed."

With a trembling hand he slowly lowered the straps of her pink tank top and undid the front clasp of her bra. He lifted her full breasts to his waiting lips and whispered, "I thought about doing this a thousand times."

Elizabeth felt the heat of his mouth on her swollen breast and tightened her grip on his broad shoulders. Desire flared across her abdomen to settle into liquid heat between her thighs. She felt his lips release her nipple. Mumbling a protest she arched her back. His breath was hot and fast as he whispered, "I thought about you naked and under me." Thumbs brushed her erect nipples. "I thought about you naked and riding me."

A trembling "Dillon" escaped her dry throat.

He heard the thickness of her voice and groaned, "Did you think of me, Elizabeth?"

"Yes."

He shifted her weight so that she was in no doubt of his arousal. "How?"

Elizabeth felt the hard column pressed against her bottom and understood his condition. It was the same as hers—on fire. They hadn't made love since that night over two weeks ago in this office. Now the need and hunger were rapidly growing out of control. The boys were upstairs playing, eight men were in the backyard working, and the fire raged on. Provocatively rocking against him she said, "I dream of you every night."

"How?" was whispered against the rapid pulse beating in her neck.

With gentle hands she cradled his head and forced his mouth lower to her aching breasts. The pressure of his lips compelled her head back as she dragged air into her starving lungs. Her voice cracked with excitement and need. "I dreamed of you doing this a thousand times." A heated tongue circled her protruding nub. "I dreamed of you naked and over me. I dreamed of you naked and under me. I dreamed of you and me alone on a deserted island, with no workmen, caterers, telephones, or kids."

"Tell me the island had sparkling white sand, crystal clear water, and you forgot to pack your bathing suit."

"Close enough." She heard the heavy thumping of the boys running down the steps and sighed. "Can Aaron sleep over tonight?"

"Definitely." With prolonged slowness Dillon fastened the front clasp of her bra and pulled the tank top up to its former position. "There's a very slim chance I might hold onto my sanity till then."

As Elizabeth scooted off his lap he felt the sway of her derriere against his bulging maleness and groaned. "Then again I might not."

With a provocative smile she opened the door. "I'll go get us something cold to drink, while you cool down." She laughed delightfully at his good-natured muttering and headed for the kitchen.

She pulled three empty ice-cube trays from the freezer before finding one that contained half a dozen frost-encrusted cubes. With a smile she filled and replaced the trays, poured root beer into two glasses, and returned to Dillon's office.

As he reached for his glass, he placed a kiss on the end of her nose. "Thank you." He watched as Elizabeth studied the blueprints on his drafting board. "That's my last job until after the wedding. Then I have two major contracts coming up." He finished his drink and set the empty glass on the corner of his desk. "I figured out a solution to our problem."

Amusement sparkled in her eyes as she saw his winning smile. "What problem is that?"

"Not enough hours in the day."

"Don't tell me, you're increasing the day to thirty hours."

Happiness shone in the depths of his eyes. "No, but close. After we're married, you can't keep baking until the wee hours of the morning. I have other plans for you."

Elizabeth watched in delight as he wiggled his eyebrows to emphasize what kind of plans he had in mind. She was so busy following his cinnamon brows that she nearly missed his next words. "I think it's time for Indescribably Delicious to expand. What do you think about opening a bakery?"

"A bakery?!"

He noted her shocked expression, mistook it for happiness, and smiled. "I know it's a big step, but I'm confident you can pull it off. Just think, you could spend the nights home with your family." Large dark eyes stared at him, and her mouth fell open. "And that's not all!"

In dread she asked, "There's more?"

"Since you'd be spending your days at your bakery and I'd be working in here, what do you think about hiring someone to help around the house?"

In silence she made her way to the French doors and pulled back the drapes. A brick walk led from the house to the center of her dream garden. The rose arbor was in place and five men were struggling with the sundial. The gardens surrounding the house were bare except for an occasional flower that survived the tangle of weeds. Her garden would have been done in time for the wedding.

Maybe Dillon needed the money. She glanced

out the door and wondered if he'd overextended himself on her wedding present. If he needed the money she'd sell her house. That should give her a couple of years home with the boys. And if need be, she'd continue baking out of Dillon's kitchen. "Can I ask a personal question?"

In a nervous gesture, he ran his fingers through his hair. Something wasn't right. "For God's sake you're going to be my wife in nine days, of course you can."

"Do we need money?"

"Money?"

"Do we need for me to work? There's nothing wrong with a wife having to work. Nowadays it's a common occurrence."

"No, you don't have to work. I can support you. We won't be rich, just middle-class comfortable."

With tear-filled eyes she turned around and faced him. "Then why are you practically throwing me out of the house and dragging in some stranger to take care of my home?"

In two strides he crossed half the room and was stopped by the look on her face. "I'm sorry, Elizabeth." He watched as a tear slid down her cheek and tried to explain. "I didn't want to tie you down with the house and the kids. I thought you'd be happier with your career."

"How could you think that?" she sobbed, crossing the room.

At the sight of the tears he'd caused, Dillon lost all sense of reason and blurted out the first thing that came to his mind. "Rachael was never happy staying home."

With a visible jerk, as if someone had slapped her, Elizabeth backed against the patio door. "I'm not Rachael." Dillon started to speak, and she quickly continued before she lost her nerve. "I think we should call off the wedding."

"Why?"

"I don't think we understand each other. It all happened too fast." Before Dillon could utter one word of protest she disappeared through the patio doors.

Dillon splashed cold water over his face and glared at the man in the mirror. He looked as if he'd been up all night. And he had. He had spent the night making frantic phone calls for reinforcements and putting the finishing touches to the apartment complex he was designing.

The sounds of his sons awakening caused him to hurry through a shower and shave. He was standing in his bedroom throwing clothes into a suitcase when his sons came in.

"Where are you going, Dad?"

"Sit down, boys. I want to talk to you." He waited for the boys to stop bouncing on his bed before sitting on the edge. "I goofed. Yesterday Elizabeth and I had a misunderstanding."

"Is that why we didn't see her and Aaron at dinner?"

"Yes. If you guys really want Elizabeth to be your stepmother and Aaron your brother, I'm going to need your help."

Kevin and Kyle glanced at each other and smiled. "Sure."

"Sometimes when adults fight, a simple 'I'm sorry' just won't do. It takes talking things out. I can't talk to Elizabeth here because she's always baking and there're too many interruptions. I'm going to take her up to the cabin and straighten things out."

"Is Aaron going to?"

"No. That's where I need your help. Uncle Shane is coming this morning to stay with you guys till Grandmom and Granddad come in from Idaho. I talked to them last night and they can't catch a plane till Saturday night. Aaron won't know Uncle Shane or your grandparents, so could you two help him out for me?"

"But, Dad, you said we could never stay with Uncle Shane again after what happened the last time."

"I know, Kevin. But this is an emergency, and Shane promised to behave himself." With a tender smile at his sons, he said, "Well, are you two going to help me?"

"Sure, Dad. Mrs. Lancaster is pretty neat. She sewed my favorite shorts for me."

Not to be outdone by his older brother, Kyle added, "Yeah, Dad, she can even cook lasagna."

He ruffled his son's hair and silently agreed she sure could cook. But not necessarily with a stove. "Come on, you two. Go get dressed. Uncle Shane will be here soon, and I want to be ready by the time he gets here."

Dillon was loading the last box of food into the van when Shane pulled up. "Well, big brother, it looks like you screwed up good this time."

"Nice to see you too, Shane."

"Need some advice?"

"Shut up and go say hello to your nephews."

Shane's chuckle followed him into the house as Dillon closed up the van. Everything was in the van except Elizabeth and her clothes. With a spring of determination in his step, he marched into his house and put operation Butterfly into motion. He was officially starting his collection.

He sent Kevin over to Aaron's with one message: Bubba was sick. In two seconds Kevin returned with Aaron fast on his heels. Dillon quickly apologized to Aaron for the fib, but he needed to talk to him. "Aaron, I would like you to meet Shane, my brother. When your mother and I get married next weekend, he'll be your uncle."

"Wow, I never had an uncle."

"Hi, Aaron."

"Hello. Will you really be my uncle?"

"You bet. I'm a pretty cool uncle, just ask Kevin and Kyle."

A chorus of agreement was heard from the boys. "Aaron, is your mom up?"

"Yeah, she's in the kitchen. But she's mad about something. She's not talking."

"How would you like to spend a couple of days here with your new uncle, Kevin, and Kyle?" Seeing the indecision in Aaron's eyes he added, "I want to take your mom away for a few days. I'm the one who got her mad and I want to make her happy again."

Aaron glanced at his new uncle and smiled. "Okay."

Dillon pulled the van in front of the cabin and forced a pleasant smile. "Are you talking to me yet?"

Elizabeth looked at the small cabin nestled under towering pines and had to admit it was as nice as he said it would be. But she wasn't telling him that; she wasn't telling him anything. She scowled at the thought of the long walk back to the nearest town as she watched him pocket the keys.

"You can scream at me now. No one will hear you."

"Do you think I care if anyone hears me?"

"Ah, she can talk."

She released her seat belt in a huff and got out of the van. She slammed the door and quickly turned toward the man rounding the front of the vehicle. "Why should I talk to you after what you did?"

"What did I do?"

"You kidnapped me. You marched uninvited into my house, threw me over your shoulder, made my son laugh at me, packed my bag, and dumped me into your van."

"I wouldn't have carried you if you had behaved."

"I told you I had to ice Mrs. Rosebloom's cake for her garden club meeting this afternoon."

"Shane volunteered to do it for you."

A look of incredibility spread across her face. "He asked where the can of icing was."

"He means well. He'll take good care of the boys until my parents get there Saturday night."

"Your parents are coming in?"

"Yeah. They heard about you wanting to back out of the wedding and figured I screwed up."

With a dejected sigh, Elizabeth walked over to the porch steps and sat down. "You didn't screw up, I did."

"How?"

"I had our whole life planned out. You'd be the bread winner and I'd get to play June Cleaver. We'd buy a new car every four years, send the boys to the best colleges, and go on a vacation every summer." She dug a trench with the toe of her sneaker and heaved a sigh. "When you mentioned the bakery and a cleaning lady, I panicked. Your dreams and mine didn't match."

A gentle finger lifted her chin. "Yes, they did. They matched perfectly, just like us. Help me unload the van and I'll explain."

"Are we really staying?"

"Till Sunday night. Longer if need be."

"Will the boys be okay?"

"Do you think I'd leave any of the boys if I thought they wouldn't be?"

"No. What about the baking I have to do?"

"Shane will handle it."

"Can he cook?"

"Who do you think taught me?"

A bubble of laughter rose in her throat. "I'd love to see the look on Mrs. Rosebloom's face when Shane delivers that cake."

Half an hour later all the food was put away, the generator started, and the windows opened. "Who's cabin is this?"

"Mine. Excuse me, ours."

"Really?"

After dumping a load of logs into the firebox next to the fireplace, he looked around the cabin with satisfaction. It was rustic and homey, with two bedrooms and a bath. The kitchen opened up into the living room, and the screened back porch begged to be sat on. "I bought it over a year ago. The boys love it here. Aaron will too."

"This is where my final exam was supposed to be, wasn't it? Not in some tent."

"Afraid so. I was going to invite you and Aaron up here this fall for a long weekend. Go put on a pair of jeans. I want to show you something."

She changed out of shorts and found herself hiking through thick pines to an unknown destination. "How much farther?"

"It's just over this rise, and for goodness' sake watch where you're walking. The last time I had you out in the woods, you nearly broke a leg."

Elizabeth climbed to the top of the rise, looked around, and caught her breath. A sparkling stream threaded its way through pine, oak, and maple trees. Dillon walked down the incline and spread out an old blanket in a small clearing by the bank. "Come sit down and enjoy the sunshine. It's supposed to rain Saturday and Sunday."

As she sat on the edge of the blanket she watched Dillon stretch out. He folded his arms under his head and stared up at the sky. "If you lie down and watch the clouds you'll see some amazing things. Look at the cloud over there. It looks like a seal with a ball on the end of its nose."

Elizabeth stared up at the cloud he pointed to. "It looks like a ballerina to me."

"How about that one? It's definitely an elephant."

"Are you out of your mind? That's a train. See the steam pouring out of its smokestack."

"That's his trunk."

"Didn't your mother ever take you to a real circus?" she asked, laughing.

"Sure, more times than she'd care to remember. I love circuses. I have to see every one that comes to town."

She was the first to break the comfortable silence as they continued to watch clouds float by. "Tell me about Rachael."

In a deep steady voice, Dillon told the story of two college sweethearts who had gotten married and lived the great yuppie dream, two different and interesting careers. Then along came Kevin and soon to follow Kyle. Rachael had put her dreams on hold for the boys and slowly, day by day, regretted it. "It was my fault. I should have listened to her when she started to complain about being smothered. I thought she was just having some bad days. I was working fourteen-hour days to reach my goal, while her dreams slipped further away."

With a sigh of regret he continued. "She once told me that she couldn't achieve her goal because she felt guilty. I didn't understand that then; I do now. She loved the boys, don't get me wrong, she just wanted more."

"And you thought I wanted more?"

"You love your business. It shows by the time and effort you put into it." He rolled onto his side and looked down into her dark eyes. "Do you want to keep on baking?"

"Not in a business. I love baking and will always be whipping up something, but that's not why I love my business. Indescribably Delicious gave me the freedom to stay home with my son."

"You don't mind the cleaning, cooking, and endless chores?"

"I'm sure there're going to be days when I'd rather be doing something else."

"Like what?"

"Gardening or reading a good book."

He tenderly traced her smiling lower lip. "I'll help around the house."

"Does this mean I don't get the maid?" she pouted.

"Maybe one day a week."

A brilliant smile lit her eyes. She watched as love and desire ignited in his eyes. "Have you ever made love while an entire circus watched?"

"No, I saved that experience for you." Sure hands undid the pink ribbon that held her braid together. He ran his fingers through the dark silken cloud and said, "Promise me one thing?"

"Anything."

"If you ever start to feel guilty or bored, tell me. We'll work it out."

Pulling his mouth down to hers, she whispered, "I will. I'm starting to get bored lying here with nothing to do."

"We'll work something out."

Dillon looked around the crowded garden hoping to spot his new bride. Wedding guests were mingling around, waiting for the bride and groom to officially start the reception. With a strained smile toward Shane, he headed into the house to locate Elizabeth. She hadn't been his wife for twenty minutes, and already he'd lost her. He was halfway across the patio when he caught a flash of pale yellow out of the corner of his eye. He changed his direction and rounded the side of the house in hopes of finding Elizabeth.

An oath escaped his lips as he spotted her with her wedding dress pulled to midthigh, kneeling and looking under the house. "What are you doing?"

"Rufus chased Snapdragon under the porch." She softly called the cat and got no response. "I don't understand it. I locked her up in my house not five minutes before the ceremony. How did she get out?"

He gently lifted her back onto her feet. "My money's on Shane."

"Don't talk to me about your brother. Do you know what he did?"

Dillon knew exactly what he'd done, but how had Elizabeth found out so fast? "What?"

"He got Bubba drunk. He fed that stupid turtle champagne."

"Lord." Silently he chalked up another one to Shane.

"Bubba's so skunked, he can't swim. He almost drowned in his pool and your father's started taking bets on whether turtles have hangovers."

So that's what all the commotion had been about on the porch. He'd been so busy trying to convince the band that Shane had hired to leave before Elizabeth saw them that he hadn't given it a second thought. How do you explain to your bride that her Victorian garden wedding was about to be invaded by an honest-to-goodness flamingo dancer. He was in the middle of a heated battle with Contessa, a sultry-eyed Spanish vixen, when his mother had told him the caterers were ready to start serving lunch.

He looked down into the lovely face of his wife and smiled. "Have I told you I loved you lately?"

Elizabeth raised her arms and pulled his mouth

down for a heated kiss. She ended the kiss with regret. All she had to do was wait till later and she'd have him all to herself. What did she care about a neurotic cat and a drunk turtle, when she could have Dillon?

With his arm anchoring her to his side, they headed back toward the reception. "So, Elizabeth McKenzie, do you like Spanish music?"

Dear Reader

We hope that you have enjoyed reading this LOVESWEPT romance.

On the following pages you will find our publishing plans for the exciting, new LOVESWEPT COLLECTION. As a discerning reader of contemporary romantic fiction you will recognise some of the LOVESWEPT authors as among the finest in the field.

Do let us know how you like our LOVESWEPT romances and if you would like further information on this wonderful series, please write to us at the following address. We look forward to hearing from you.

The Editors
Loveswept
Bantam Books
61–63 Uxbridge Road
EALING
London W5 5SA

THE LOVESWEPT COLLECTION

THE LOVESWEPT COLLECTION

THE LOVESWEPT COLLECTION

July 1991

No. 41 0553 44051 9 **TENDER SAVAGE**
by Iris Johansen

No. 42 0553 44052 7 **SOME ENCHANTED SEASON**
by Patricia Burroughs

No. 43 0553 44053 5 **WIFE FOR HIRE**
by Janet Evanovich

No. 44 0553 44056 X **MEN OF ICE: FROZEN IDOLS**
by Helen Mittermeyer

August 1991

No. 45 0553 44057 8 **ONCE UPON A TIME: THE LADY AND THE
LION** by Kay Hooper

No. 46 0553 44058 6 **SATIN SHEETS AND STRAWBERRIES**
by Marcia Evanick

No. 47 0553 44060 8 **STORMING THE CASTLE**
by Joan Elliott Pickart

No. 48 0553 44062 4 **SWEET AND WILDE**
by Billie Green

September 1991

No. 49 0553 44012 8 **VALLEY OF FIRE**
by Peggy Webb

No. 50 0553 44023 3 **ADAM'S OUTLAW**
by Sandra Chastain

No. 51 0553 44032 2 **JINX**
by Courtney Henke

No. 52 0553 44027 6 **LOVIN' A GOOD OL' BOY**
by Mary Kay McComas

THE LOVESWEPT COLLECTION

Published by
Bantam Books